# CHRISTMAS EVE
# ON LONESOME

## BY THE SAME AUTHOR

**Christmas Eve on Lonesome.** Illustrated. $1.50.

**The Little Shepherd of Kingdom Come.** Illustrated. $1.50.

**Crittenden.** A Kentucky Story of Love and War. $1.50.

**The Kentuckians.** A Novel. Illustrated. $1.25.

**A Cumberland Vendetta.** A Novel. Illustrated. $1.25.

**A Mountain Europa.** $1.25.

**"Hell fer Sartain,"** and Other Stories. $1.00.

**Blue Grass and Rhododendron.** Outdoor Life in Kentucky. Illustrated. $1.75 *net*.

# CHRISTMAS EVE ON LONESOME

## AND OTHER STORIES

BY

JOHN FOX, Jr.

ILLUSTRATED

CHARLES SCRIBNER'S SONS

NEW YORK :: 1904

Buck saw the shadowed gesture of an arm, and he cocked his pistol.

TO

THOMAS  NELSON  PAGE

# CONTENTS

# ILLUSTRATIONS

# CHRISTMAS EVE ON LONESOME

# CHRISTMAS EVE ON LONESOME

IT was Christmas Eve on Lonesome. But nobody on Lonesome knew that it was Christmas Eve, although a child of the outer world could have guessed it, even out in those wilds where Lonesome slipped from one lone log-cabin high up the steeps, down through a stretch of jungled darkness to another lone cabin at the mouth of the stream.

There was the holy hush in the gray twilight that comes only on Christmas Eve. There were the big flakes of snow that fell as they never fall except on Christmas Eve. There was a snowy man on horseback in a big coat, and with saddle-pockets that

[ 3 ]

might have been bursting with toys for children in the little cabin at the head of the stream.

But not even he knew that it was Christmas Eve. He was thinking of Christmas Eve, but it was of Christmas Eve of the year before, when he sat in prison with a hundred other men in stripes, and listened to the chaplain talk of peace and good-will to all men upon earth, when he had forgotten all men upon earth but one, and had only hatred in his heart for him.

"Vengeance is mine!" saith the Lord.

That was what the chaplain had thundered at him. And then, as now, he thought of the enemy who had betrayed him to the law, and had sworn away his liberty, and had robbed him of everything in life except a fierce longing for the day when he could strike back and strike to kill.

And then, while he looked back hard into the chaplain's eyes, and now, while he splashed through the yellow mud thinking of that Christmas Eve, Buck shook his head; and then, as now, his sullen heart answered:

"Mine!"

The big flakes drifted to crotch and twig and limb. They gathered on the brim of Buck's slouch hat, filled out the wrinkles in his big coat, whitened his hair and his long mustache, and sifted into the yellow, twisting path that guided his horse's feet.

High above he could see through the whirling snow now and then the gleam of a red star. He knew it was the light from his enemy's window; but somehow the chaplain's voice kept ringing in his ears, and every time he saw the light he couldn't help thinking of the story of the Star that

[ 5 ]

the chaplain told that Christmas Eve, and he dropped his eyes by and by, so as not to see it again, and rode on until the light shone in his face.

Then he led his horse up a little ravine and hitched it among the snowy holly and rhododendrons, and slipped toward the light. There was a dog somewhere, of course; and like a thief he climbed over the low rail-fence and stole through the tall snow-wet grass until he leaned against an apple-tree with the sill of the window two feet above the level of his eyes.

Reaching above him, he caught a stout limb and dragged himself up to a crotch of the tree. A mass of snow slipped softly to the earth. The branch creaked above the light wind; around the corner of the house a dog growled and he sat still.

He had waited three long years and he

[ 6 ]

had ridden two hard nights and lain out two cold days in the woods for this.

And presently he reached out very carefully, and noiselessly broke leaf and branch and twig until a passage was cleared for his eye and for the point of the pistol that was gripped in his right hand.

A woman was just disappearing through the kitchen door, and he peered cautiously and saw nothing but darting shadows. From one corner a shadow loomed suddenly out in human shape. Buck saw the shadowed gesture of an arm, and he cocked his pistol. That shadow was his man, and in a moment he would be in a chair in the chimney-corner to smoke his pipe, maybe—his last pipe.

Buck smiled—pure hatred made him smile—but it was mean, a mean and sorry thing to shoot this man in the back, dog

[ 7 ]

though he was; and now that the moment had come a wave of sickening shame ran through Buck. No one of his name had ever done that before; but this man and his people had, and with their own lips they had framed palliation for him. What was fair for one was fair for the other, they always said. A poor man couldn't fight money in the courts; and so they had shot from the brush, and that was why they were rich now and Buck was poor—why his enemy was safe at home, and he was out here, homeless, in the apple-tree.

Buck thought of all this, but it was no use. The shadow slouched suddenly and disappeared; and Buck was glad. With a gritting oath between his chattering teeth he pulled his pistol in and thrust one leg down to swing from the tree—he would meet him face to face next day and kill him

[ 8 ]

like a man—and there he hung as rigid as though the cold had suddenly turned him, blood, bones, and marrow, into ice.

The door had opened, and full in the firelight stood the girl who he had heard was dead. He knew now how and why that word was sent him. And now she who had been his sweetheart stood before him—the wife of the man he meant to kill.

Her lips moved—he thought he could tell what she said: "Git up, Jim, git up!" Then she went back.

A flame flared up within him now that must have come straight from the devil's forge. Again the shadows played over the ceiling. His teeth grated as he cocked his pistol, and pointed it down the beam of light that shot into the heart of the apple-tree, and waited.

[ 9 ]

The shadow of a head shot along the rafters and over the fireplace. It was a madman clutching the butt of the pistol now, and as his eye caught the glinting sight and his heart thumped, there stepped into the square light of the window—a child!

It was a boy with yellow tumbled hair, and he had a puppy in his arms. In front of the fire the little fellow dropped the dog, and they began to play.

"Yap! yap! yap!"

Buck could hear the shrill barking of the fat little dog, and the joyous shrieks of the child as he made his playfellow chase his tail round and round or tumbled him head over heels on the floor. It was the first child Buck had seen for three years; it was *his* child and *hers;* and, in the apple-tree, Buck watched fixedly.

They were down on the floor now, rolling over and over together; and he watched them until the child grew tired and turned his face to the fire and lay still—looking into it. Buck could see his eyes close presently, and then the puppy crept closer, put his head on his playmate's chest, and the two lay thus asleep.

And still Buck looked—his clasp loosening on his pistol and his lips loosening under his stiff mustache—and kept looking until the door opened again and the woman crossed the floor. A flood of light flashed suddenly on the snow, barely touching the snow-hung tips of the apple-tree, and he saw her in the doorway—saw her look anxiously into the darkness—look and listen a long while.

Buck dropped noiselessly to the snow when she closed the door. He wondered

[ 11 ]

what they would think when they saw his tracks in the snow next morning; and then he realized that they would be covered before morning.

As he started up the ravine where his horse was he heard the clink of metal down the road and the splash of a horse's hoofs in the soft mud, and he sank down behind a holly-bush.

Again the light from the cabin flashed out on the snow.

"That you, Jim?"

"Yep!"

And then the child's voice: "Has oo dot thum tandy?"

"Yep!"

The cheery answer rang out almost at Buck's ear, and Jim passed death waiting for him behind the bush which his left foot brushed, shaking the snow from the red

[ 12 ]

berries down on the crouching figure beneath.

Once only, far down the dark jungled way, with the underlying streak of yellow that was leading him whither, God only knew—once only Buck looked back. There was the red light gleaming faintly through the moonlit flakes of snow. Once more he thought of the Star, and once more the chaplain's voice came back to him.

"Mine!" saith the Lord.

Just how, Buck could not see with himself in the snow and *him* back there for life with her and the child, but some strange impulse made him bare his head.

"Yourn," said Buck grimly.

But nobody on Lonesome—not even Buck—knew that it was Christmas Eve.

[ 13 ]

# THE ARMY OF THE CALLAHAN

# THE ARMY OF THE CALLAHAN

## I

THE dreaded message had come. The lank messenger, who had brought it from over Black Mountain, dropped into a chair by the stove and sank his teeth into a great hunk of yellow cheese. "Flitter Bill" Richmond waddled from behind his counter, and out on the little platform in front of his cross-roads store. Out there was a group of earth-stained countrymen, lounging against the rickety fence or swinging on it, their heels clear of the ground, all whittling, chewing, and talking the matter over. All looked up at Bill, and he looked down at them, running his eye keenly from one to another until he came to one powerful young fellow loosely bent over a wagon-tongue. Even on him, Bill's eyes stayed but a moment, and then were lifted higher in anxious thought.

The message had come at last, and the man who brought it had heard it fall from Black Tom's own lips. The "wild Jay-Hawkers of Kaintuck" were coming over into Virginia to get Flitter Bill's store, for they were mountain Unionists and Bill was a valley rebel and lawful prey. It was past belief. So long had he prospered, and so well, that Bill had come to feel that he sat safe in the hollow of God's hand. But he now must have protection—and at once—from the hand of man.

Roaring Fork sang lustily through the rhododendrons. To the north yawned "the Gap" through the Cumberland

Mountains. "Callahan's Nose," a huge gray rock, showed plain in the clear air, high above the young foliage, and under it, and on up the rocky chasm, flashed Flitter Bill's keen mind, reaching out for help.

Now, from Virginia to Alabama the Southern mountaineer was a Yankee, because the national spirit of 1776, getting fresh impetus in 1812 and new life from the Mexican War, had never died out in the hills. Most likely it would never have died out, anyway; for, the world over, any seed of character, individual or national, that is once dropped between lofty summits brings forth its kind, with deathless tenacity, year after year. Only, in the Kentucky mountains, there were more slaveholders than elsewhere in the mountains of the South. These, naturally,

[ 19 ]

fought for their slaves, and the division
thus made the war personal and terrible
between the slaveholders who dared to
stay at home, and the Union "Home
Guards" who organized to drive them
away. In Bill's little Virginia valley, of
course, most of the sturdy farmers had
shouldered Confederate muskets and gone
to the war. Those who had stayed at home
were, like Bill, Confederate in sympathy,
but they lived in safety down the valley,
while Bill traded and fattened just opposite the Gap, through which a wild road
ran over into the wild Kentucky hills.
Therein Bill's danger lay; for, just at
this time, the Harlan Home Guard under
Black Tom, having cleared those hills,
were making ready, like the Pict and Scot
of olden days, to descend on the Virginia
valley and smite the lowland rebels at

the mouth of the Gap. Of the "stay-at-homes," and the deserters roundabout, there were many, very many, who would "stand in" with any man who would keep their bellies full, but they were well-nigh worthless even with a leader, and, without a leader, of no good at all. Flitter Bill must find a leader for them, and anywhere than in his own fat self, for a leader of men Bill was not born to be, nor could he see a leader among the men before him. And so, standing there one early morning in the spring of 1865, with uplifted gaze, it was no surprise to him—the coincidence, indeed, became at once one of the articles of perfect faith in his own star—that he should see afar off, a black slouch hat and a jogging gray horse rise above a little knoll that was in line with the mouth of the Gap. At once he

[ 21 ]

crossed his hands over his chubby stomach with a pious sigh, and at once a plan of action began to whirl in his little round head. Before man and beast were in full view the work was done, the hands were unclasped, and Flitter Bill, with a chuckle, had slowly risen, and was waddling back to his desk in the store.

It was a pompous old buck who was bearing down on the old gray horse, and under the slouch hat with its flapping brim—one Mayhall Wells, by name. There were but few strands of gray in his thick blue-black hair, though his years were rounding half a century, and he sat the old nag with erect dignity and perfect ease. His bearded mouth showed vanity immeasurable, and suggested a strength of will that his eyes—the real seat of power—denied, for, while shrewd and

[ 22 ]

keen, they were unsteady.  In reality, he was a great coward, though strong as an ox, and whipping with ease every man who could force him into a fight.  So that, in the whole man, a sensitive observer would have felt a peculiar pathos, as though nature had given him a desire to be, and no power to become, and had then sent him on his zigzag way, never to dream wherein his trouble lay.

"Mornin', gentle*men* !"

"Mornin', Mayhall !"

All nodded and spoke except Hence Sturgill on the wagon-tongue, who stopped whittling, and merely looked at the big man with narrowing eyes.

Tallow Dick, a yellow slave, appeared at the corner of the store, and the old buck beckoned him to come and hitch his horse. Flitter Bill had reappeared on the stoop with a piece of white paper in his hand. The lank messenger sagged in the doorway behind him, ready to start for home.

"Mornin', *Captain* Wells," said Bill, with great respect. Every man heard the title, stopped his tongue and his knifeblade, and raised his eyes; a few smiled— Hence Sturgill grinned. Mayhall stared, and Bill's left eye closed and opened with lightning quickness in a most portentous wink. Mayhall straightened his shoulders —seeing the game, as did the crowd at once: Flitter Bill was impressing that messenger in case he had some dangerous card up his sleeve.

"*Captain* Wells," Bill repeated significantly, "I'm sorry to say yo' new uniform has not arrived yet. I am expecting it to-morrow." Mayhall toed the line with soldierly promptness.

[ 24 ]

"Well, I'm sorry to hear that, suh—
sorry to hear it, suh," he said, with slow,
measured speech. "My men are comin'
in fast, and you can hardly realize er—er
what it means to an old soldier er—er not
to have—er—" And Mayhall's answering wink was portentous.

"My friend here is from over in Kain-
tucky, and the Harlan Home Gyard over
there, he says, is a-making some threats."

Mayhall laughed.

"So I have heerd—so I have heerd."
He turned to the messenger. "We shall
be ready fer 'em, suh, ready fer 'em with
a thousand men—one thousand men, suh,
right hyeh in the Gap—right hyeh in the
Gap. Let 'em come on—let 'em come
on!" Mayhall began to rub his hands
together as though the conflict were close
at hand, and the mountaineer slapped one

thigh heartily. "Good for you! Give 'em hell!" He was about to slap Mayhall on the shoulder and call him "pardner," when Flitter Bill coughed, and Mayhall lifted his chin.

"Captain Wells?" said Bill.

"Captain Wells," repeated Mayhall with a stiff salutation, and the messenger from over Black Mountain fell back with an apologetic laugh. A few minutes later both Mayhall and Flitter Bill saw him shaking his head, as he started homeward toward the Gap. Bill laughed silently, but Mayhall had grown grave. The fun was over and he beckoned Bill inside the store.

"Misto Richmond," he said, with hesitancy and an entire change of tone and manner, "I am afeerd I ain't goin' to be able to pay you that little amount I

owe you, but if you can give me a little
mo' time——"

"Captain Wells," interrupted Bill slowly, and again Mayhall stared hard at him,
"as betwixt friends, as have been pus-
sonal friends fer nigh onto twenty year,
I hope you won't mention that little
matter to me ag'in—until I mentions it to
you."

"But, Misto Richmond, Hence Sturgill
out thar says as how he heerd you say
that if I didn't pay——"

"*Captain* Wells," interrupted Bill again
and again Mayhall stared hard—it was
strange that Bill could have formed the
habit of calling him "Captain" in so short
a time—"yestiddy is not to-day, is it?
And to-day is not to-morrow? I axe you
—have I said one word about that little
matter *to-day?* Well, borrow not from

yestiddy nor to-morrow, to make trouble fer to-day. There is other things fer to-day, Captain Wells."

Mayhall turned here.

"Misto Richmond," he said, with great earnestness, "you may not know it, but three times since thet long-legged jay-hawker's been gone you hev plainly—and if my ears do not deceive me, an' they never hev—you have plainly called me '*Captain* Wells.' I knowed yo' little trick whilst he was hyeh, fer I knowed whut the feller had come to tell ye; but since he's been gone, three times, Misto Rich-mond——"

"Yes," drawled Bill, with an unction that was strangely sweet to Mayhall's wondering ears, "an' I do it ag'in, *Captain* Wells."

"An' may I axe you," said Mayhall,

[ 28 ]

ruffling a little, "may I axe you—why
you——"

"Certainly," said Bill, and he handed
over the paper that he held in his hand.

Mayhall took the paper and looked it
up and down helplessly—Flitter Bill slyly
watching him.

Mayhall handed it back. "If you
please, Misto Richmond—I left my specs
at home." Without a smile, Bill began.
It was an order from the commandant at
Cumberland Gap, sixty miles farther down
Powell's Valley, authorizing Mayhall
Wells to form a company to guard the
Gap and to protect the property of Confederate citizens in the valley; and a commission of captaincy in the said company
for the said Mayhall Wells. Mayhall's
mouth widened to the full stretch of his
lean jaws, and, when Bill was through

[ 29 ]

reading, he silently reached for the paper and looked it up and down and over and over, muttering:

"Well—well—well!" And then he pointed silently to the name that was at the bottom of the paper.

Bill spelled out the name:

*"Jefferson Davis,"* and Mayhall's big fingers trembled as he pulled them away, as though to avoid further desecration of that sacred name. Then he rose, and a magical transformation began that can be likened—I speak with reverence—to the turning of water into wine. Captain Mayhall Wells raised his head, set his chin well in, and kept it there. He straightened his shoulders, and kept them straight. He paced the floor with a tread that was martial, and once he stopped before the door with his right hand thrust under his

breast-pocket, and with wrinkling brow studied the hills. It was a new man— with the water in his blood changed to wine—who turned suddenly on Flitter Bill Richmond:

"I can collect a vehy large force in a vehy few days." Flitter Bill knew that— that he could get together every loafer between the county-seat of Wise and the county-seat of Lee—but he only said encouragingly:

"Good!"

"An' we air to pertect the property— *I* am to pertect the property of the Confederate citizens of the valley—that means *you*, Misto Richmond, and *this store*."

Bill nodded.

Mayhall coughed slightly. "There is one thing in the way, I opine. Whar—I axe you—air we to git somethin' to eat

[ 31 ]

fer my command?" Bill had anticipated this.

"I'll take keer o' that."

Captain Wells rubbed his hands.

"Of co'se, of co'se—you are a soldier and a patriot—you can afford to feed 'em as a slight return fer the pertection I shall give you and yourn."

"Certainly," agreed Bill dryly, and with a prophetic stir of uneasiness.

"Vehy—vehy well. I shall begin *now,* Misto Richmond." And, to Flitter Bill's wonder, the captain stalked out to the stoop, announced his purpose with the voice of an auctioneer, and called for volunteers then and there. There was dead silence for a moment. Then there was a smile here, a chuckle there, an incredulous laugh, and Hence Sturgill, "bully of the Pocket," rose from the wagon-tongue, closed his knife, came slowly forward, and cackled his scorn straight up into the teeth of Captain Mayhall Wells. The captain looked down and began to shed his coat.

"I take it, Hence Sturgill, that you air laughin' at me?"

"I am a-laughin' at *you,* Mayhall Wells," he said, contemptuously, but he was surprised at the look on the good-natured giant's face.

*"Captain* Mayhall Wells, ef you please."

"Plain ole Mayhall Wells," said Hence, and Captain Wells descended with no little majesty and "biffed" him.

The delighted crowd rose to its feet and gathered around. Tallow Dick came running from the barn. It was biff—biff, and biff again, but not nip and tuck for long. Captain Mayhall closed in. Hence Sturgill struck the earth like a Homeric pine, and the captain's mighty arm played above him and fell, resounding. In three minutes Hence, to the amazement of the crowd, roared:

" 'Nough!"

But Mayhall breathed hard and said quietly:

*"Captain* Wells!" Hence shouted.

"Plain ole—" But the captain's huge fist was poised in the air over his face.

"Capt'n Wells," he growled, and the captain rose and calmly put on his coat, while the crowd looked respectful, and Hence Sturgill staggered to one side, as though beaten in spirit, strength, and wits as well. The captain beckoned Flitter Bill inside the store. His manner had a distinct savor of patronage.

[ 34 ]

Captain Wells descended with no little majesty and "biffed" him.

"Misto Richmond," he said, "I make you—I appoint you, by the authority of Jefferson Davis and the Confederate States of Ameriky, as commissary-gineral of the Army of the Callahan."

"As *what?*" Bill's eyes blinked at the astounding dignity of his commission.

"Gineral Richmond, I shall not repeat them words." And he didn't, but rose and made his way toward his old gray mare. Tallow Dick held his bridle.

"Dick," he said, jocosely, "goin' to run away ag'in?" The negro almost paled, and then, with a look at a blacksnake whip that hung on the barn door, grinned.

"No, suh—no, suh—'deed I ain't, suh —no mo'."

Mounted, the captain dropped a three-cent silver piece in the negro's startled hand. Then he vouchsafed the wondering Flitter Bill and the gaping crowd a military salute and started for the yawning mouth of the Gap—riding with shoulders squared and chin well in—riding as should ride the commander of the Army of the Callahan.

Flitter Bill dropped his blinking eyes to the paper in his hand that bore the commission of Jefferson Davis and the Confederate States of America to Mayhall Wells of Callahan, and went back into his store. He looked at it a long time and then he laughed, but without much mirth.

## II

GRASS had little chance to grow for three weeks thereafter under the cowhide boots of Captain Mayhall Wells. When the twentieth morning came over the hills, the mists parted over the Stars and Bars floating from the top of a tall poplar up through the Gap and flaunting brave defiance to Black Tom, his Harlan Home Guard, and all other jay-hawking Unionists of the Kentucky hills. It parted over the Army of the Callahan asleep on its arms in the mouth of the chasm, over Flitter Bill sitting, sullen and dejected, on the stoop of his store; and over Tallow Dick stealing corn-bread from the kitchen to make ready for flight that night through the Gap, the mountains, and to the yellow river that was the Mecca of the runaway slave.

At the mouth of the Gap a ragged private stood before a ragged tent, raised a long dinner-horn to his lips, and a mighty blast rang through the hills, reveille! And out poured the Army of the Callahan from shack, rock-cave, and coverts of sticks and leaves, with squirrel rifles, Revolutionary muskets, shot-guns, clasp-knives, and horse-pistols for the duties of the day under Lieutenant Skaggs, tactician, and Lieutenant Boggs, quondam terror of Roaring Fork.

That blast rang down the valley into Flitter Bill's ears and startled him into action. It brought Tallow Dick's head out of the barn door and made him grin.

"Dick!" Flitter Bill's call was sharp and angry.

"Yes, suh!"

"Go tell ole Mayhall Wells that I ain't goin' to send him nary another pound o' bacon an' nary another tin-cup o' meal— no, by ——, I ain't."

Half an hour later the negro stood before the ragged tent of the commander of the Army of the Callahan.

"Marse Bill say he ain't gwine to sen' you no mo' rations—no mo'."

"*What!*"

Tallow Dick repeated his message and the captain scowled—mutiny!

"Fetch my hoss!" he thundered.

Very naturally and very swiftly had the trouble come, for straightway after the captain's fight with Hence Sturgill there had been a mighty rally to the standard of Mayhall Wells. From Pigeon's Creek the loafers came—from Roaring Fork,

Cracker's Neck, from the Pocket down the valley, and from Turkey Cove. Recruits came so fast, and to such proportions grew the Army of the Callahan, that Flitter Bill shrewdly suggested at once that Captain Wells divide it into three companies and put one up Pigeon's Creek under Lieutenant Jim Skaggs and one on Callahan under Lieutenant Tom Boggs, while the captain, with a third, should guard the mouth of the Gap. Bill's idea was to share with those districts the honor of his commissary-generalship; but Captain Wells crushed the plan like a dried puff-ball.

"Yes," he said, with fine sarcasm. "What will them Kanetuckians do *then?* Don't you know, Gineral Richmond? Why, I'll tell you what they'll do. They'll jest swoop down on Lieutenant Boggs and gobble him up. Then they'll swoop down

[ 40 ]

on Lieutenant Skaggs on Pigeon and gobble him up. Then they'll swoop down on me and gobble me up. No, they won't gobble *me* up, but they'll come damn nigh it. An' what kind of a report will I make to Jeff Davis, Gineral Richmond? *Captured in detail,* suh? No, suh. I'll jest keep Lieutenant Boggs and Lieutenant Skaggs close by me, and we'll pitch our camp right here in the Gap whar we can pertect the property of Confederate citizens and be close to our base o' supplies, suh. That's what *I'll* do!"

"Gineral" Richmond groaned, and when in the next breath the mighty captain casually inquired if *that uniform of his* had come yet, Flitter Bill's fat body nearly rolled off his chair.

"You will please have it here next Monday," said the captain, with great firmness.

[ 41 ]

"It is necessary to the proper discipline of my troops." And it was there the following Monday—a regimental coat, gray jeans trousers, and a forage cap that Bill purchased from a passing Morgan raider. Daily, orders would come from Captain Wells to General Flitter Bill Richmond to send up more rations, and Bill groaned afresh when a man from Callahan told how the captain's family was sprucing up on meal and flour and bacon from the captain's camp. Humiliation followed. It had never occurred to Captain Wells that being a captain made it incongruous for him to have a "general" under him, until Lieutenant Skaggs, who had picked up a manual of tactics somewhere, cautiously communicated his discovery. Captain Wells saw the point at once. There was but one thing to do—to reduce General Richmond to the ranks—and it was done. Technically, thereafter, the general was purveyor for the Army of the Callahan, but to the captain himself he was—gallingly to the purveyor—simple Flitter Bill.

The strange thing was that, contrary to his usual shrewdness, it should have taken Flitter Bill so long to see that the difference between having his store robbed by the Kentucky jay-hawkers and looted by Captain Wells was the difference between tweedle-dum and tweedle-dee, but, when he did see, he forged a plan of relief at once. When the captain sent down Lieutenant Boggs for a supply of rations, Bill sent the saltiest, rankest bacon he could find, with a message that he wanted to see the great man. As before, when Captain Wells rode down to the store, Bill handed out a piece of paper, and, as before, the captain had left his "specs" at home. The paper was an order that, whereas the distinguished services of Captain Wells to the Confederacy were appreciated by Jefferson Davis, the said Captain Wells was, and is, hereby empowered to duly, and in accordance with the tactics of war, impress what live-stock he shall see fit and determine fit for the good of his command. The news was joy to the Army of the Callahan. Before it had gone the rounds of the camp Lieutenant Boggs had spied a fat heifer browsing on the edge of the woods and ordered her surrounded and driven down. Without another word, when she was close enough, he raised his gun and would have shot her dead in her tracks had he not been arrested by a yell of command and horror from his superior.

"Air you a-goin' to have me cashiered and shot, Lieutenant Boggs, fer violatin' the ticktacks of war?" roared the captain, indignantly. "Don't you know that I've got to *impress* that heifer accordin' to the rules an' regulations? Git roun' that heifer." The men surrounded her. "Take her by the horns. Now! In the name of Jefferson Davis and the Confederate States of Ameriky, I hereby and hereon do duly impress this heifer for the purposes and use of the Army of the Callahan, so help me God! Shoot her down, Bill Boggs, shoot her down!"

Now, naturally, the soldiers preferred fresh meat, and they got it—impressing cattle, sheep, and hogs, geese, chickens, and ducks, vegetables—nothing escaped the capacious maw of the Army of the Callahan. It was a beautiful idea, and the success of it pleased Flitter Bill mightily, but the relief did not last long. An indignant murmur rose up and down valley and creek bottom against the outrages, and one angry old farmer took a pot-shot at Captain Wells with a squirrel rifle, clipping the visor of his forage cap; and from that day the captain began to call with immutable regularity again on Flitter Bill for bacon and meal. That morning the last straw fell in a demand for a wagonload of rations to be delivered before noon, and, worn to the edge of his patience, Bill had sent a reckless refusal. And now he was waiting on the stoop of his store, looking at the mouth of the Gap and waiting for it to give out into the valley Captain Wells and his old gray mare. And at last, late in the afternoon, there was the captain coming—coming at a swift gallop

—and Bill steeled himself for the on-slaught like a knight in a joust against a charging antagonist. The captain saluted stiffly—pulling up sharply and making no move to dismount.

"Purveyor," he said, "Black Tom has just sent word that he's a-comin' over hyeh this week—have you heerd that, purveyor?" Bill was silent.

"Black Tom says you *air* responsible for the Army of the Callahan. Have you heerd that, purveyor?" Still was there silence.

"He says he's a-goin' to hang me to that poplar whar floats them Stars and Bars"—Captain Mayhall Wells chuckled —"an' he says he's a-goin' to hang *you* thar fust, though; have you heerd *that,* purveyor?"

The captain dropped the titular address

now, and threw one leg over the pommel of his saddle.

"Flitter Bill Richmond," he said, with great nonchalance, "I axe you—do you prefer that I should disband the Army of the Callahan, or do you not?"

"No."

The captain was silent a full minute, and his face grew stern. "Flitter Bill Richmond, I had no idee o' disbandin' the Army of the Callahan, but do you know what I did aim to do?" Again Bill was silent.

"Well, suh, I'll tell you whut I aim to do. If you don't send them rations I'll have you cashiered for mutiny, an' if Black Tom don't hang you to that air poplar, I'll hang you thar myself, suh; yes, by ——, I will. Dick!" he called sharply to the slave. "Hitch up that air wagon, fill hit full o' bacon and meal, and drive it up thar to my tent. An' be mighty damn quick about it, or I'll hang you, too."

The negro gave a swift glance to his master, and Flitter Bill feebly waved acquiescence.

"Purveyor, I wish you good-day."

Bill gazed after the great captain in dazed wonder (was this the man who had come cringing to him only a few short weeks ago?) and groaned aloud.

But for lucky or unlucky coincidence, how could the prophet ever have gained name and fame on earth?

Captain Wells rode back to camp chuckling—chuckling with satisfaction and pride; but the chuckle passed when he caught sight of his tent. In front of

it were his lieutenants and some half a
dozen privates, all plainly in great agita-
tion, and in the midst of them stood the
lank messenger who had brought the first
message from Black Tom, delivering another from the same source. Black Tom
*was* coming, coming sure, and unless that
flag, that "Rebel Rag," were hauled down
under twenty-four hours, Black Tom would
come over and pull it down, and to that
same poplar hang "Captain Mayhall an'
his whole damn army." Black Tom might
do it anyhow—just for fun.

While the privates listened the captain
strutted and swore; then he rested his hand
on his hip and smiled with silent sarcasm,
and then swore again—while the respectful lieutenants and the awed soldiery of
the Callahan looked on. Finally he
spoke.

[ 50 ]

"Ah—when did Black Tom say that?" he inquired casually.

"Yestiddy mornin'. He said he was goin' to start over hyeh early this mornin'." The captain whirled.

"What? Then why didn't you git over hyeh *this* mornin'?"

"Couldn't git across the river last night."

"Then he's a-comin' to-day?"

"I reckon Black Tom'll be hyeh in about two hours—mebbe he ain't fer away now." The captain was startled.

Lieutenant Skaggs," he called, sharply, "git yo' men out thar an' draw 'em up in two rows!"

The face of the student of military tactics looked horrified. The captain in his excitement had relaxed into language that was distinctly agricultural, and, catching

[ 51 ]

the look on his subordinate's face, and at the same time the reason for it, he roared, indignantly:

"Air you afeer'd, sir? Git yo' men out, I said, an' march 'em up thar in front of the Gap. Lieutenant Boggs, take ten men an' march at double quick through the Gap, an' defend that poplar with yo' life's blood. If you air overwhelmed by superior numbers, fall back, suh, step by step until you air re-enforced by Lieutenant Skaggs. If you two air not able to hold the enemy in check, you may count on me an' the Army of the Callahan to grind *him*—" (How the captain, now thoroughly aroused to all the fine terms of war, did roll that technical "him" under his tongue) —"to grind him to pieces ag'in them towerin' rocks, and plunge him in the bilin' waters of Roarin' Fawk. Forward, suh—

[ 52 ]

double quick." Lieutenant Skaggs touched his cap. Lieutenant Boggs looked embarrassed and strode nearer.

"Captain, whar am I goin' to git ten men to face them Kanetuckians?"

"Whar air they goin' to git a off'cer to lead 'em, you'd better say," said the captain, severely, fearing that some of the soldiers had heard the question. "If you air afeer'd, suh"—and then he saw that no one had heard, and he winked—winked with most unmilitary familiarity.

"Air you a good climber, Lieutenant Boggs?" Lieutenant Boggs looked mystified, but he said he was.

"Lieutenant Boggs, I now give you the opportunity to show yo' profound knowledge of the ticktacks of war. You may now be guilty of disobedience of ordahs, and I will not have you court-martialled for

[ 53 ]

the same. In other words, if, after a survey of the situation, you think best—why," the captain's voice dropped to a hoarse whisper, "pull that flag down, Lieutenant Boggs, pull her down."

# III

It was an hour by sun now. Lieutenant Boggs and his devoted band of ten were making their way slowly and watchfully up the mighty chasm—the lieutenant with his hand on his sword and his head bare, and bowed in thought. The Kentuckians were on their way—at that moment they might be riding full speed toward the mouth of Pigeon, where floated the flag. They might gobble him and his command up when they emerged from the Gap. Suppose they caught him up that tree. His command might escape, but *he* would be up there, saving them the trouble of stringing him up. All they would have to do would be to send up after him a man with a rope, and let him drop. That was enough. Lieutenant Boggs called a halt and explained the real purpose of the expedition.

"We will wait here till dark," he said, "so them Kanetuckians can't ketch us, whilst we are climbing that tree."

And so they waited opposite Bee Rock, which was making ready to blossom with purple rhododendron. And the reserve back in the Gap, under Lieutenant Skaggs, waited. Waited, too, the Army of the Callahan at the mouth of the Gap, and waited restlessly Captain Wells at the door of his tent, and Flitter Bill on the stoop of his store—waited everybody but Tallow Dick, who, in the general confusion, was slipping through the rhododendrons along

[ 56 ]

the bank of Roaring Fork, until he could climb the mountain-side and slip through the Gap high over the army's head.

What could have happened?

When dusk was falling, Captain Wells dispatched a messenger to Lieutenant Skaggs and his reserve, and got an answer; Lieutenant Skaggs feared that Boggs had been captured without the firing of a single shot—but the flag was floating still. An hour later, Lieutenant Skaggs sent another message—he could not see the flag. Captain Wells answered, stoutly:

"Hold yo' own."

And so, as darkness fell, the Army of the Callahan waited in the strain of mortal expectancy as one man; and Flitter Bill waited, with his horse standing saddled in the barn, ready for swift flight. And, as darkness fell, Tallow Dick was cautiously

[ 57 ]

picking his way alongside the steep wall of the Gap toward freedom, and picking it with stealthy caution, foot by foot; for up there, to this day, big loose rocks mount half way to the jagged points of the black cliffs, and a careless step would have detached one and sent an avalanche of rumbling stones down to betray him. A single shot rang suddenly out far up through the Gap, and the startled negro sprang forward, slipped, and, with a low, frightened oath, lay still. Another shot followed, and another. Then a hoarse murmur rose, loudened into thunder, and ended in a frightful—boom! One yell rang from the army's throat:

"The Kentuckians! The Kentuckians! The wild, long-haired, terrible Kentuckians!"

Captain Wells sprang into the air.

[ 58 ]

"My God, they've got a cannon!"

Then there was a martial chorus—the crack of rifle, the hoarse cough of horse-pistol, the roar of old muskets.

"Bing! Bang! Boom! Bing—bing! Bang—bang! Boom—boom! Bing—bang—boom!"

Lieutenant Skaggs and his reserves heard the beat of running feet down the Gap.

"They've gobbled Boggs," he said, and the reserve rushed after him as he fled. The army heard the beat of their coming feet.

"They've gobbled Skaggs," the army said.

Then was there bedlam as the army fled —a crashing through bushes—a splashing into the river, the rumble of mule-wagons, yells of terror, swift flying shapes through

[ 59 ]

the pale moonlight. Flitter Bill heard the din as he stood by his barn door.

"They've gobbled the army," said Flitter Bill, and he, too, fled like a shadow down the valley.

Nature never explodes such wild and senseless energy as when she lets loose a mob in a panic. With the army, it was each man for himself and devil take the hindmost; and the flight of the army was like a flight from the very devil himself. Lieutenant Boggs, whose feet were the swiftest in the hills, outstripped his devoted band. Lieutenant Skaggs, being fat and slow, fell far behind his reserve, and dropped exhausted on a rock for a moment to get his breath. As he rose, panting, to resume flight, a figure bounded out of the darkness behind him, and he gathered it in silently and went with it to the ground,

[ 60 ]

where both fought silently in the dust until they rolled into the moonlight and each looked the other in the face.

"That you, Jim Skaggs?"

"That you, Tom Boggs?"

Then the two lieutenants rose swiftly, but a third shape bounded into the road— a gigantic figure—Black Tom! With a startled yell they gathered him in—one by the waist, the other about the neck, and, for a moment, the terrible Kentuckian —it could be none other—swung the two clear of the ground, but the doughty lieutenants hung to him. Boggs trying to get his knife and Skaggs his pistol, and all went down in a heap.

"I surrender—I surrender!" It was the giant who spoke, and at the sound of his voice both men ceased the struggle, and, strange to say, no one of the three laughed.

[ 61 ]

"Lieutenant Boggs," said Captain Wells, thickly, "take yo' thumb out o' my mouth. Lieutenant Skaggs, leggo my leg an' stop bitin' me."

"Sh—sh—sh—" said all three.

The faint swish of bushes as Lieutenant Boggs's ten men scuttled into the brush behind them—the distant beat of the army's feet getting fainter ahead of them, and then silence—dead, dead silence.

"Sh—sh—sh!"

\* \* \* \* \*

With the red streaks of dawn Captain Mayhall Wells was pacing up and down in front of Flitter Bill's store, a gaping crowd about him, and the shattered remnants of the army drawn up along Roaring Fork in the rear. An hour later Flitter Bill rode calmly in.

"I stayed all night down the valley,"

[ 62 ]

said Flitter Bill. "Uncle Jim Richmond was sick. I hear you had some trouble last night, Captain Wells." The captain expanded his chest.

"Trouble!" he repeated, sarcastically. And then he told how a charging horde of dare-devils had driven him from camp with overwhelming numbers and one piece of artillery; how he had rallied the army and fought them back, foot by foot, and put them to fearful rout; how the army had fallen back again just when the Kentuckians were running like sheep, and how he himself had stayed in the rear with Lieutenant Boggs and Lieutenant Skaggs, "to cover their retreat, suh," and how the purveyor, if he would just go up through the Gap, would doubtless find the cannon that the enemy had left behind in their flight. It was just while he was thus telling the

[ 63 ]

tale for the twentieth time that two figures appeared over the brow of the hill and drew near—Hence Sturgill on horseback and Tallow Dick on foot.

"I ketched this nigger in my corn-fiel' this mornin'," said Hence, simply, and Flitter Bill glared, and without a word went for the blacksnake ox-whip that hung by the barn door.

For the twenty-first time Captain Wells started his tale again, and with every pause that he made for breath Hence cackled scorn.

"An', Hence Sturgill, ef you will jus' go up in the Gap you'll find a cannon, captured, suh, by me an' the Army of the Callahan, an'——"

"Cannon!" Hence broke in. "Speak up, nigger!" And Tallow Dick spoke up—grinning:

[ 64 ]

"Speak up, nigger."

"I done it!"

"What!" shouted Flitter Bill.

"I kicked a rock loose climbin' over Callahan's nose."

Bill dropped his whip with a chuckle of pure ecstasy. Mayhall paled and stared. The crowd roared, the Army of the Callahan grinned, and Hence climbed back on his horse.

"Mayhall Wells," he said, "plain ole Mayhall Wells, I'll see you on Couht Day. I ain't got time now."

And he rode away.

# IV

THAT day Captain Mayhall Wells and the Army of the Callahan were in disrepute. Next day the awful news of Lee's surrender came. Captain Wells refused to believe it, and still made heroic effort to keep his shattered command together. Looking for recruits on Court Day, he was twitted about the rout of the army by Hence Sturgill, whose long-coveted chance to redeem himself had come. Again, as several times before, the captain declined to fight—his health was essential to the general well-being—but Hence laughed in his face, and the captain had to face the music, though the heart of him was gone.

He fought well, for he was fighting for

his all, and he knew it. He could have whipped with ease, and he did whip, but the spirit of the thoroughbred was not in Captain Mayhall Wells. He had Sturgill down, but Hence sank his teeth into Mayhall's thigh while Mayhall's hands grasped his opponent's throat. The captain had only to squeeze, as every rough-and-tumble fighter knew, and endure his pain until Hence would have to give in. But Mayhall was not built to endure. He roared like a bull as soon as the teeth met in his flesh, his fingers relaxed, and to the disgusted surprise of everybody he began to roar with great distinctness and agony:

" 'Nough! 'Nough!"

The end was come, and nobody knew it better than Mayhall Wells. He rode home that night with hands folded on the

[ 67 ]

pommel of his saddle and his beard crushed by his chin against his breast. For the last time, next morning he rode down to Flitter Bill's store. On the way he met Parson Kilburn and for the last time Mayhall Wells straightened his shoulders and for one moment more resumed his part: perhaps the parson had not heard of his fall.

"Good-mornin', parsing," he said, pleasantly. "Ah—where have you been?" The parson was returning from Cumberland Gap, whither he had gone to take the oath of allegiance.

"By the way, I have something here for you which Flitter Bill asked me to give you. He said it was from the commandant at Cumberland Gap."

"Fer me?" asked the captain—hope springing anew in his heart. The parson

[ 68 ]

handed him a letter. Mayhall looked at it upside down.

"If you please, parsing," he said, handing it back, "I hev left my specs at home."

The parson read that, whereas Captain Wells had been guilty of grave misdemeanors while in command of the Army of the Callahan, he should be arrested and court-martialled for the same, or be given the privilege of leaving the county in twenty-four hours. Mayhall's face paled a little and he stroked his beard.

"Ah—does anybody but you know about this ordah, parsing?"

"Nobody."

"Well, if you will do me the great favor, parsing, of not mentioning it to nary a living soul—as fer me and my ole gray hoss and my household furniture—we'll be

[ 69 ]

in Kanetuck afore daybreak to-morrow mornin'!" And he was.

But he rode on just then and presented himself for the last time at the store of Flitter Bill. Bill was sitting on the stoop in his favorite posture. And in a moment there stood before him plain Mayhall Wells—holding out the order Bill had given the parson that day.

"Misto Richmond," he said, "I have come to tell you good-by."

Now just above the selfish layers of fat under Flitter Bill's chubby hands was a very kind heart. When he saw Mayhall's old manner and heard the old respectful way of address, and felt the dazed helplessness of the big beaten man, the heart thumped.

"I am sorry about that little amount I owe you; I think I'll be able shortly—"

[ 70 ]

But Bill cut him short. Mayhall Wells, beaten, disgraced, driven from home on charge of petty crimes, of which he was undoubtedly guilty, but for which Bill knew he himself was responsible—Mayhall on his way into exile and still persuading himself and, at that moment, almost persuading him that he meant to pay that little debt of long ago—was too much for Flitter Bill, and he proceeded to lie—lying with deliberation and pleasure.

"Captain Wells," he said—and the emphasis on the title was balm to Mayhall's soul—"you have protected me in time of war, an' you air welcome to yo' uniform an' you air welcome to that little debt. Yes," he went on, reaching down into his pocket and pulling out a roll of bills, "I tender you in payment for that same protection the regular pay of a officer in the

Confederate service"—and he handed out
the army pay for three months in Confederate greenbacks—"an' five dollars in
money of the United States, of which I
an', doubtless, you, suh, air true and loyal
citizens. Captain Wells, I bid you good-
by an' I wish ye well—I wish ye well."

From the stoop of his store Bill watched
the captain ride away, drooping at the
shoulders, and with his hands folded on
the pommel of his saddle—his dim blue
eyes misty, the jaunty forage cap a mock-
ery of his iron-gray hair, and the flaps of
his coat fanning either side like mournful
wings.

And Flitter Bill muttered to himself:

"Atter he's gone long enough fer these
things to blow over, I'm going to bring him
back and give him another chance—yes,
damme if I don't git him back."

[72]

And Bill dropped his remorseful eye to the order in his hand. Like the handwriting of the order that lifted Mayhall like magic into power, the handwriting of this order, that dropped him like a stone—was Flitter Bill's own.

# THE LAST STETSON

# THE LAST STETSON

## I

A MIDSUMMER freshet was running over old Gabe Bunch's waterwheel into the Cumberland. Inside the mill Steve Marcum lay in one dark corner with a slouched hat over his face. The boy Isom was emptying a sack of corn into the hopper. Old Gabe was speaking his mind.

Always the miller had been a man of peace; and there was one time when he thought the old Stetson-Lewallen feud was done. That was when Rome Stetson, the last but one of his name, and Jasper Lewallen, the last but one of his, put their guns down and fought with bare fists on a high ledge above old Gabe's mill one morning at daybreak. The man who was beaten was to leave the mountains; the other was to stay at home and have peace. Steve Marcum, a Stetson, heard the sworn terms and saw the fight. Jasper was fairly whipped; and when Rome let him up he proved treacherous and ran for his gun. Rome ran too, but stumbled and fell. Jasper whirled with his Winchester and was about to kill Rome where he lay, when a bullet came from somewhere and dropped him back to the ledge again. Both Steve Marcum and Rome Stetson said they had not fired the shot; neither would say who had. Some thought one man was lying, some thought the other was, and Jasper's death lay between the two. State troops came then, under the Governor's order, from the Blue Grass, and Rome had to drift down the river one night in old Gabe's canoe and on out of the mountains for good. Martha Lewallen, who, though Jasper's sister, and the last of the name, loved and believed Rome, went with him. Marcums and Braytons who had taken sides in the fight hid in the bushes around Hazlan, or climbed over into Virginia. A railroad started up the Cumberland. "Furriners" came in to buy wild lands and get out timber. Civilization began to press over the mountains and down on Hazlan, as it had pressed in on Breathitt, the seat of another feud, in another county. In Breathitt the feud was long past, and with good reason old Gabe thought that it was done in Hazlan.

But that autumn a panic started over from England. It stopped the railroad far down the Cumberland; it sent the "furri-

ners" home, and drove civilization back.
Marcums and Braytons came in from hiding, and drifted one by one to the old fight-
ing-ground. In time they took up the old
quarrel, and with Steve Marcum and Steve
Brayton as leaders, the old Stetson-Lewallen feud went on, though but one soul was
left in the mountains of either name.
That was Isom, a pale little fellow whom
Rome had left in old Gabe's care; and he,
though a Stetson and a half-brother to
Rome, was not counted, because he was
only a boy and a foundling, and because
his ways were queer.

There was no open rupture, no organized
division—that might happen no more.
The mischief was individual now, and am-
bushing was more common. Certain men
were looking for each other, and it was a
question of "drawin' quick 'n' shootin'"

quick" when the two met by accident, or
of getting the advantage "from the bresh."

In time Steve Marcum had come face to
face with old Steve Brayton in Hazlan,
and the two Steves, as they were known,
drew promptly. Marcum was in the dust
when the smoke cleared away; and now,
after three months in bed, he was just out
again. He had come down to the mill to
see Isom. This was the miller's first chance
for remonstrance, and, as usual, he began
to lay it down that every man who had
taken a human life must sooner or later
pay for it with his own. It was an old
story to Isom, and, with a shake of impa-
tience, he turned out the door of the mill,
and left old Gabe droning on under his
dusty hat to Steve, who, being heavy with
moonshine, dropped asleep.

Outside the sun was warm, the flood was

calling from the dam, and the boy's petu-
lance was gone at once. For a moment he
stood on the rude platform watching the
tide; then he let one bare foot into the
water, and, with a shiver of delight,
dropped from the boards. In a moment
his clothes were on the ground behind a
laurel thicket, and his slim white body was
flashing like a faun through the reeds and
bushes up stream. A hundred yards away
the creek made a great loop about a wet
thicket of pine and rhododendron, and he
turned across the bushy neck. Creeping
through the gnarled bodies of rhododendron, he dropped suddenly behind the pine,
and lay flat in the black earth. Ten yards
through the dusk before him was the half-
bent figure of a man letting an old army
haversack slip from one shoulder; and
Isom watched him hide it with a rifle under

[ 82 ]

a bush, and go noiselessly on towards the road. It was Crump, Eli Crump, who had been a spy for the Lewallens in the old feud and who was spying now for old Steve Brayton. It was the second time Isom had seen him lurking about, and the boy's impulse was to hurry back to the mill. But it was still peace, and without his gun Crump was not dangerous; so Isom rose and ran on, and, splashing into the angry little stream, shot away like a roll of birch bark through the tawny crest of a big wave. He had done the feat a hundred times; he knew every rock and eddy in flood-time, and he floated through them and slipped like an eel into the mill-pond. Old Gabe was waiting for him.

"Whut ye mean, boy," he said, sharply, "reskin' the fever an' ager this way? No wonder folks thinks ye air half crazy. Git

inter them clothes now 'n' come in hyeh.
You'll ketch yer death o' cold swimmin'
this way atter a fresh."

The boy was shivering when he took his
seat at the funnel, but he did not mind that;
some day he meant to swim over that dam.
Steve still lay motionless in the corner near
him, and Isom lifted the slouched hat and
began tickling his lips with a straw. Steve
was beyond the point of tickling, and Isom
dropped the hat back and turned to tell the
miller what he had seen in the thicket. The
dim interior darkened just then, and Crump
stood in the door. Old Gabe stared hard
at him without a word of welcome, but
Crump shuffled to a chair unasked, and sat
like a toad astride it, with his knees close
up under his arms, and his wizened face in
his hands. Meeting Isom's angry glance,
he shifted his own uneasily.

"Seed the new preacher comin' 'long to-day?" he asked. Drawing one dirty finger across his forehead, "Got a long scar 'cross hyeh."

The miller shook his head.

"Well, he's a-comin'. I've been waitin' fer him up the road, but I reckon I got to git 'cross the river purty soon now."

Crump had been living over in Breathitt since the old feud. He had been "convicted" over there by Sherd Raines, a preacher from the Jellico Hills, and he had grown pious. Indeed, he had been trailing after Raines from place to place, and he was following the circuit-rider now to the scene of his own deviltry—Hazlan.

"Reckon you folks don't know I got the cirkit-rider to come over hyeh, do ye?" he went on. "Ef he can't preach! Well, I'd tell a man! He kin jus' draw the heart

[ 85 ]

out'n a holler log! He 'convicted' me fust
night, over thar in Breathitt. He come
up thar, ye know, to stop the feud, he said;
'n' thar was laughin' from one eend o'
Breathitt to t'other; but thar was the whop-
pinest crowd thar I ever see when he did
come. The meetin'-house wasn't big
enough to hold 'em, so he goes out on the
aidge o' town, 'n' climbs on to a stump.
He hed a woman with him from the settle-
mints—she's a-waitin' at Hazlan fer him
now—'n' she had a cur'us little box, 'n' he
put her 'n' the box on a big rock, 'n' started
in a callin' 'em his bretherin' 'n' sisteren,
'n' folks seed mighty soon thet he meant
it, too. He's always mighty easylike, tell
he gits to the blood-penalty."

At the word, Crump's listeners paid sudden heed. Old Gabe's knife stopped short
in the heart of the stick he was whittling;

the boy looked sharply up from the running meal into Crump's face and sat
still.

"Well, he jes prayed to the Almighty as
though he was a-talkin' to him face to face,
'n' then the woman put her hands on that
box, 'n' the sweetes' sound anybody thar
ever heerd come outen it. Then she got
to singin'. Hit wusn't nuthin' anybody
thar'd ever heerd; but some o' the women
folks was a snifflin' 'fore she got through.
He pitched right into the feud, as he calls
hit, 'n' the sin o' sheddin' human blood, I
tell ye; 'n' 'twixt him and the soldiers I
reckon thar won't be no more fightin' in
Breathitt. He says, 'n' he always says it
mighty loud"—Crump raised his own
voice—"thet the man as kills his feller-
critter hev some day got ter give up his
own blood, sartin 'n' *shore.*"

[ 87 ]

It was old Gabe's pet theory, and he was nodding approval. The boy's parted lips shook with a spasm of fear, and were as quickly shut tight with suspicion. Steve raised his head as though he too had heard the voice, and looked stupidly about him.

"I tol' him," Crump went on, "thet things was already a-gettin' kind o' frolicsome round hyeh agin; thet the Marcums 'n' Braytons was a-takin' up the ole war, 'n' would be a-plunkin' one 'nother every time they got together, 'n' a-gittin' the whole country in fear 'n' tremblin'—now thet Steve Marcum had come back."

Steve began to scowl and a vixenish smile hovered at Isom's lips.

"He knows mighty well—fer I tol' him —thet thar hain't a wuss man in all these mountains than thet very Steve—" The name ended in a gasp, and the wizened

[ 88 ]

gossip was caught by the throat and tossed, chair and all, into a corner of the mill.

"None o' that, Steve!" called the miller, sternly. "Not hyeh. Don't hurt him now!"

Crump's face stiffened with such terror that Steve broke into a laugh.

"Well, ye air a skeery critter!" he said, contemptuously. "I hain't goin' to hurt him, Uncl' Gabe, but he must be a plumb idgit, a-talkin' 'bout folks to thar face, 'n' him so puny an' spindlin'! You git!"

Crump picked himself up trembling— "Don't ye ever let me see ye on this side o' the river agin, now"—and shuffled out, giving Marcum one look of fear and unearthly hate.

"Convicted!" snorted Steve. "I heerd old Steve Brayton had hired him to layway me, 'n' I swar I believe hit's so."

"Well, he won't hev to give him more'n a chaw o' tobaccer now," said Gabe. "He'll come purty near doin' hit hisself, I reckon, ef he gits the chance."

"Well, he kin git the chance ef I gits my leetle account settled with ole Steve Brayton fust. 'Pears like that old hog ain't satisfied shootin' me hisself." Stretching his arms with a yawn, Steve winked at Isom and moved to the door. The boy followed him outside.

"We're goin' fer ole Brayton about the dark o' the next moon, boy," he said. "He's sort o' s'picious now, 'n' we'll give him a leetle time to git tame. I'll have a bran'-new Winchester fer ye, Isom. Hit ull be like ole times agin, when Rome was hyeh. Whut's the matter, boy?" he asked, suddenly. Isom looked unresponsive, listless.

"Air ye gittin' sick agin?"

"Well, I hain't feelin' much peert, Steve."

"Take keer o' yourself, boy. Don't git sick *now*. We'll have to watch Eli Crump purty close. I don't know why I hain't killed thet spyin' skunk long ago, 'ceptin' I never had a shore an' sartin reason fer doin' it."

Isom started to speak then and stopped. He would learn more first; and he let Steve go on home unwarned.

The two kept silence after Marcum had gone. Isom turned away from old Gabe, and stretched himself out on the platform. He looked troubled. The miller, too, was worried.

"Jus' a hole in the groun'," he said, half to himself; "that's whut we're all comin' to! 'Pears like we mought help one 'nother to keep out'n hit, 'stid o' holpin' 'em in."

Brown shadows were interlacing out in the mill-pond, where old Gabe's eyes were intent. A current of cool air had started down the creek to the river. A katydid began to chant. Twilight was coming, and the miller rose.

"Hit's a comfort to know *you* won't be mixed up in all this devilment," he said; and then, as though he had found more light in the gloom: "Hit's a comfort to know the new rider air shorely a-preachin' the right doctrine, 'n' I want ye to go hear him. Blood fer blood—life fer a life! Your grandad shot ole Tom Lewallen in Hazlan. Ole Jack Lewallen shot him from the bresh. Tom Stetson killed ole Jack; ole Jass killed Tom, 'n' so hit comes down, fer back as I can ricollect. I hev

[ 92 ]

*nuver* knowed hit to fail." The lad had risen on one elbow. His face was pale and uneasy, and he averted it when the miller turned in the door.

"You'd better stay hyeh, son, 'n' finish up the grist. Hit won't take long. Hev ye got victuals fer yer supper?"

Isom nodded, without looking around, and when old Gabe was gone he rose nervously and dropped helplessly back to the floor.

" 'Pears like old Gabe knows I killed Jass," he breathed, sullenly. 'Pears like all of 'em knows hit, 'n' air jus' a-torment-in' me."

Nobody dreamed that the boy and his old gun had ended that fight on the cliff; and without knowing it, old Gabe kept the lad in constant torture with his talk of the blood-penalty. But Isom got used to it in

time, for he had shot to save his brother's
life. Steve Marcum treated him thereafter as an equal. Steve's friends, too,
changed in manner towards him because
Steve had. And now, just when he had
reached the point of wondering whether,
after all, there might not be one thing that
old Gabe did not know, Crump had come
along with the miller's story, which he had
got from still another, a circuit-rider, who
must know the truth. The fact gave him
trouble.

"Mebbe hit's goin' to happen when I
goes with Steve atter ole Brayton," he
mumbled, and he sat thinking the matter
over, until a rattle and a whir inside the
mill told him that the hopper was empty.
He arose to fill it, and coming out again,
he heard hoof-beats on the dirt road. A
stranger rode around the rhododendrons

[ 94 ]

and shouted to him, asking the distance to
Hazlan. He took off his hat when Isom
answered, to wipe the dust and perspiration from his face, and the boy saw a white
scar across his forehead. A little awe-
stricken, the lad walked towards him.

"Air you the new rider whut's goin' to
preach up to Hazlan?" he asked.

Raines smiled at the solemnity of the
little fellow. "Yes," he said, kindly.
"Won't you come up and hear me?"

"Yes, sir," he said, and his lips parted
as though he wanted to say something else,
but Raines did not notice.

"I wished I had axed him," he said,
watching the preacher ride away. "Uncle
Gabe knows might' nigh ever'thing, 'n' he
says so. Crump said the rider said so;
but Crump might 'a' been lyin'. He 'most
al'ays is. I wished I had axed *him*."

[ 95 ]

Mechanically the lad walked along the mill-race, which was made of hewn boards and hollow logs. In every crevice grass hung in thick bunches to the ground or tipped wiry blades over the running water. Tightening a prop where some silvery jet was getting too large, he lifted the tail-gate a trifle and lay down again on the platform near the old wheel. Out in the mill-pond the water would break now and then into ripples about some unwary moth, and the white belly of a fish would flash from the surface. It was the only sharp accent on the air. The chant of the katydids had become a chorus, and the hush of darkness was settling over the steady flow of water and the low drone of the millstones.

"I hain't afeerd," he kept saying to himself. "I hain't afeerd o' nothin' nor no-*body;*" but he lay brooding until his head throbbed, until darkness filled the narrow gorge, and the strip of dark blue up through the trees was pointed with faint stars. He was troubled when he rose, and climbed on Rome's horse and rode home-ward—so troubled that he turned finally and started back in a gallop for Hazlan.

It was almost as Crump had said. There was no church in Hazlan, and, as in Breath-itt, the people had to follow Raines outside the town, and he preached from the road-side. The rider's Master never had a tabernacle more simple: overhead the stars and a low moon; close about, the trees still and heavy with summer; a pine torch over his head like a yellow plume; two tallow dips hung to a beech on one side, and flick-ing to the other the shadows of the people who sat under them. A few Marcums and Braytons were there, one faction shadowed

[ 97 ]

on Raines's right, one on his left. Between
them the rider stood straight, and prayed
as though talking with some one among
the stars. Behind him the voice of the
woman at her tiny organ rose among the
leaves. And then he spoke as he had
prayed; and from the first they listened like
children, while in their own homely speech
he went on to tell them, just as he would
have told children, a story that some of
them had never heard before. "Forgive
your enemies as He had forgiven his,"
that was his plea. Marcums and Braytons
began to press in from the darkness on each
side, forgetting each other as the rest of
the people forgot them. And when the
story was quite done, Raines stood a full
minute without a word. No one was prepared for what followed. Abruptly his
voice rose sternly—"Thou shalt not kill";

and then Satan took shape under the torch. The man was transformed, swaying half crouched before them. The long black hair fell across the white scar, and picture after picture leaped from his tongue with such vividness that a low wail started through the audience, and women sobbed in their bonnets. It was penalty for bloodshed—not in this world: penalty eternal in the next; and one slight figure under the dips staggered suddenly aside into the darkness.

It was Isom; and no soul possessed of devils was ever more torn than his, when he splashed through Troubled Fork and rode away that night. Half a mile on he tried to keep his eyes on his horse's neck, anywhere except on one high gray rock to which they were raised against his will— the peak under which he had killed young

[ 99 ]

Jasper. There it was staring into the moon, but watching him as he fled through the woods, shuddering at shadows, dodging branches that caught at him as he passed, and on in a run, until he drew rein and slipped from his saddle at the friendly old mill. There was no terror for him there. There every bush was a friend; every beech trunk a sentinel on guard for him in shining armor.

It was the old struggle that he was starting through that night—the old fight of humanity from savage to Christian; and the lad fought it until, with the birth of his wavering soul, the premonitions of the first dawn came on. The patches of moonlight shifted, paling. The beech columns mottled slowly with gray and brown. A ruddy streak was cleaving the east like a slow sword of fire. The chill air began to pulse and the mists to stir. Moisture had gathered on the boy's sleeve. His horse was stamping uneasily, and the lad rose stiffly, his face gray but calm, and started home. At old Gabe's gate he turned in his saddle to look where, under the last sinking star, was once the home of his old enemies. Farther down, under the crest, was old Steve Brayton, alive, and at that moment perhaps asleep.

"Forgive your enemies;" that was the rider's plea. Forgive old Steve, who had mocked him, and had driven Rome from the mountains; who had threatened old Gabe's life, and had shot Steve Marcum almost to death! The lad drew breath quickly, and standing in his stirrups, stretched out his fist, and let it drop, slowly.

## II

OLD Gabe was just starting out when Isom reached the cabin, and the old man thought the boy had been at the mill all night. Isom slept through the day, and spoke hardly a word when the miller came home, though the latter had much to say of Raines, the two Steves, and of the trouble possible. He gave some excuse for not going with old Gabe the next day, and instead went into the woods alone.

Late in the middle of the afternoon he reached the mill. Old Gabe sat smoking outside the door, and Isom stretched himself out on the platform close to the water, shading his eyes from the rich sunlight with one ragged sleeve.

"Uncl' Gabe," he said, suddenly, "s'posin' Steve Brayton was to step out'n the bushes thar some mawnin' 'n' pull down his Winchester on ye, would ye say, 'Lawd, fergive him, fer he don't know whut he do'?"

Old Gabe had told him once about a Stetson and a Lewallen who were heard half a mile away praying while they fought each other to death with Winchesters. There was no use "prayin' an' shootin'," the miller declared. There was but one way for them to escape damnation; that was to throw down their guns and make friends. But the miller had forgotten, and his mood that morning was whimsical.

"Well, I mought, Isom," he said, "ef I didn't happen to have a gun handy."

The humor was lost on Isom. His chin was moving up and down, and his face was

serious. That was just it. He could forgive Jass—Jass was dead; he could forgive Crump, if he caught him in no devilment; old Brayton even—after Steve's revenge was done. But now— The boy
rose, shaking his head.

"Uncl' Gabe," he said with sudden passion, "whut ye reckon Rome's a-doin'?"

The miller looked a little petulant.
"Don't ye git tired axin' me thet question,
Isom? Rome's a-scratchin' right peert fer
a livin', I reckon, fer hisself 'n' Marthy.
Yes, 'n' mebbe fer a young 'un too by this
time. Ef ye air honin' fer Rome, why
don't ye rack out 'n' go to him? Lawd
knows I'd hate ter see ye go, but I tol'
Rome I'd let ye whenever ye got ready, 'n'
so I will."

Isom had no answer, and old Gabe was
puzzled. It was always this way. The

boy longed for Rome, the miller could see. He spoke of him sometimes with tears, and sometimes he seemed to be on the point of going to him, but he shrank inexplicably when the time for leaving came.

Isom started into the mill now without a word, as usual. Old Gabe noticed that his feet were unsteady, and with quick remorse began to question him.

"Kinder puny, hain't ye, Isom?"

"Well, I hain't feelin' much peert."

"Hit was mighty keerless," old Gabe said, with kindly reproach, "swimmin' the crick atter a fresh."

"Hit wasn't the swimmin'," he protested, dropping weakly at the threshold. "Hit was settin' out 'n the woods. I was in Hazlan t'other night, Uncl' Gabe, to hear the new rider."

The miller looked around with quick in-

terest. "I've been skeered afore by riders
a-tellin' 'bout the torments o' hell, but I
never heerd nothin' like his tellin' 'bout the
Lord. He said the Lord was jes as pore
as anybody thar, and lived jes as rough;
thet He made fences and barns 'n' ox-yokes
'n' sech like, an' He couldn't write His own
name when He started out to save the
worl'; an' when he come to the p'int whar
His enemies tuk hol' of Him, the rider jes
crossed his fingers up over his head 'n' axed
us if we didn't know how it hurt to run a
splinter into a feller's hand when he's log-
gin', or a thorn into yer foot when ye're
goin' barefooted.

"Hit jes made me sick, Uncl' Gabe,
hearin' him tell how they stretched Him
out on a cross o' wood, when He'd come
down fer nothin' but to save 'em, 'n' stuck
a spear big as a co'n-knife into His side, 'n'

give Him vinegar, 'n' let Him hang thar
'n' die, with His own mammy a-standin'
down on the groun' a-cryin' 'n' watchin'
Him. Some folks thar never heerd sech
afore. The women was a-rockin', 'n' ole
Granny Day axed right out ef thet tuk
place a long time ago; 'n' the rider said,
'Yes, a long time ago, mos' two thousand
years.' Granny was a-cryin', Uncl' Gabe,
'n' she said, sorter soft, 'Stranger, let's hope
that hit hain't so'; 'n' the rider says, 'But
hit air so; 'n' He fergive 'em *while they
was doin' it.*' Thet's whut got me, Uncl'
Gabe, 'n' when the woman got to singin',
somethin' kinder broke loose hyeh"—Isom
passed his hand over his thin chest—" 'n' I
couldn't git breath. I was mos' afeerd to
ride home. I jes layed at the mill studyin',
till I thought my head would bust. I reckon hit was the Sperit a-workin' me. Looks

like I was mos' convicted, Uncl' Gabe."
His voice trembled and he stopped.
"Crump *was* a-lyin'," he cried, suddenly.
"But hit's wuss, Uncl' Gabe; hit's wuss!
You say a life fer a life in *this* worl'; the
rider says hit's in the *next,* 'n' I'm mis'ble,
Uncl' Gabe. Ef Rome—I wish Rome was
hyeh," he cried, helplessly. "I don't know
whut to do."

The miller rose and limped within the
mill, and ran one hand through the shifting
corn. He stood in the doorway, looking
long and perplexedly towards Hazlan; he
finally saw, he thought, just what the lad's
trouble was. He could give him some comfort, and he got his chair and dragged it
out to the door across the platform, and sat
down in silence.

"Isom," he said at last, "the Sperit air
shorely a-workin' ye, 'n' I'm glad of it.

But ye mus'n't worry about the penalty a-fallin' on Rome. Steve Marcum killed Jass—he can't fool me—'n' I've told Steve he's got thet penalty to pay ef he gits up this trouble. I'm glad the Sperit's a-workin' ye, but ye mus'n't worry 'bout Rome."

Isom rose suddenly on one elbow, and with a moan lay back and crossed his arms over his face.

Old Gabe turned and left him.

"Git up, Isom." It was the miller's voice again, an hour later. "You better go home now. Ride the hoss, boy," he added, kindly.

Isom rose, and old Gabe helped him mount, and stood at the door. The horse started, but the boy pulled him to a standstill again.

"I want to ax ye jes one thing more,

Uncl' Gabe," he said, slowly. "S'posin'
Steve had a-killed Jass to keep him from
killin' Rome, hev he got to be damned fer
it jes the same? Hev he got to give up
eternal life anyways? Hain't thar no way
out'n it—no way?"

There was need for close distinction now
and the miller was deliberate.

"Ef Steve shot Jass," he said, "jes to
save Rome's life—he had the right to shoot
him. Thar hain't no doubt 'bout that. The
law says so. But"—there was a judicial
pause—"I've heerd Steve say that he hated
Jass wuss 'n anybody on earth, 'cept old
Brayton; 'n' ef he wus glad o' the chance
o' killin' him, why— the Lord air merciful,
Isom; the Bible air true, 'n' hit says an 'eye
fer an eye 'n' a tooth fer a tooth,' 'n' I
never knowed hit to fail—but the Lord air
merciful. Ef Steve would only jes repent,

'n' ef, 'stid o' fightin' the Lord by takin' human life, he'd fight fer Him by savin' it, I reckon the Lord would fergive him. Fer ef ye lose yer life fer Him, He do say you'll find it agin somewhar—sometime."

Old Gabe did not see the sullen despair that came into the boy's tense face. The subtlety of the answer had taken the old man back to the days when he was magistrate, and his eyes were half closed. Isom rode away without a word. From the dark of the mill old Gabe turned to look after him again.

"I'm afeerd he's a-gittin' feverish agin. Hit looks like he's convicted; but"—he knew the wavering nature of the boy—"I don't know—I don't know."

Going home an hour later, the old man saw several mountaineers climbing the path towards Steve Marcum's cabin; it meant

[ 111 ]

the brewing of mischief; and when he
stopped at his own gate, he saw at the bend
of the road a figure creep from the bushes
on one side into the bushes on the other.

It looked like Crump.

# III

IT was Crump, and fifty yards behind him was Isom, slipping through the brush after him—Isom's evil spirit—old Gabe, Raines, "conviction," blood-penalty, forgotten, all lost in the passion of a chase which has no parallel when the game is man.

Straight up the ravine Crump went along a path which led to Steve Marcum's cabin. There was a clump of rhododendron at the head of the ravine, and near Steve's cabin. About this hour Marcum would be chopping wood for supper, or sitting out in his porch in easy range from the thicket. Crump's plan was plain: he was about his revenge early, and Isom was exultant.

"Oh, no, Eli, you won't git Steve this time.   Oh, naw!"

The bushes were soon so thick that he could no longer follow Crump by sight, and every few yards he had to stop to listen, and then steal on like a mountain-cat towards the leaves rustling ahead of him. Half-way up the ravine Crump turned to the right and stopped. Puzzled, Isom pushed so close that the spy, standing irresolute on the edge of the path, whirled around. The boy sank to his face, and in a moment footsteps started and grew faint; Crump had darted across the path, and was running through the undergrowth up the spur. Isom rose and hurried after him; and when, panting hard, he reached the top, the spy's skulking figure was sliding from Steve's house and towards the Breathitt road; and with a hot, puzzled face, the boy went down after it.

[ 114 ]

On a little knob just over a sudden turn in the road Crump stopped, and looking sharply about him, laid his gun down. Just in front of him were two rocks, waist-high, with a crevice between them. Drawing a long knife from his pocket, he climbed upon them, and began to cut carefully away the spreading top of a bush that grew on the other side. Isom crawled down towards him like a lizard, from tree to tree. A moment later the spy was filling up the crevice with stones, and Isom knew what he was about; he was making a "blind" to waylay Steve, who, the boy knew, was going to Breathitt by that road the next Sunday. How did Crump know that— how did he know everything? The crevice filled, Crump cut branches and stuck them between the rocks. Then he pushed his rifle through the twigs, and taking aim several times, withdrew it. When he

turned away at last and started down to the
road, he looked back once more, and Isom
saw him grinning. Almost chuckling in
answer, the lad slipped around the knob
to the road the other way, and Crump
threw up his gun with a gasp of fright
when a figure rose out of the dusk before
him.

"Hol' on, Eli!" said Isom, easily.
"Don't git skeered! Hit's nobody but me.
Whar ye been?"

Crump laughed, so quick was he disarmed of suspicion. "Jes up the river a
piece to see Aunt Sally Day. She's a fust
cousin o' mine by marriage."

Isom's right hand was slipping back as
if to rest on his hip. "D'you say you'd
been 'convicted,' Eli?"

Crump's answer was chantlike. "Yes,
Lawd, reckon I have."

"Goin' to stop all o' yer lyin', air ye," Isom went on, in the same tone, and Crump twitched as though struck suddenly from behind, "an' stealin' 'n' *lay-wayin'?*"

"Look a-hyeh, boy——" he began, roughly, and mumbling a threat, started on.

"Uh, Eli!" Even then the easy voice fooled him again, and he turned. Isom had a big revolver on a line with his breast. "Drap yer gun!" he said, tremulously.

Crump tried to laugh, but his guilty face turned gray. "Take keer, boy," he gasped; "yer gun's cocked. Take keer, I tell ye!"

"Drap it, damn ye!" Isom called in sudden fury, "'n' git clean away from it!" Crump backed, and Isom came forward and stood with one foot on the fallen Winchester.

"I seed ye, Eli. Been makin' a blind fer Steve, hev ye? Goin' to shoot him in the

[ 117 ]

back, too, air ye? You're ketched at last,
Eli. You've done a heap o' devilment.
You're gittin' wuss all the time. You
oughter be dead, 'n' now——"

Crump found voice in a cry of terror
and a whine for mercy. The boy looked
at him, unable to speak his contempt.

"Git down thar!" he said, finally; and
Crump, knowing what was wanted,
stretched himself in the road. Isom sat
down on a stone, the big pistol across one
knee.

"Roll over!" Crump rolled at full
length.

"Git up!" Isom laughed wickedly.
"Ye don't look purty, Eli." He lifted the
pistol and nipped a cake of dirt from the
road between Crump's feet. With another
cry of fear, the spy began a vigorous dance.

"Hol' on, Eli; I don't want ye to dance.

Ye belong to the chu'ch now, 'n' I wouldn't
have ye go agin yer religion fer nothin'.
Stan' still!" Another bullet and another
cut between Crump's feet. " 'Pears like
ye don't think I kin shoot straight. Eli,"
he went on, reloading the empty chambers,
"some folks think I'm a idgit, 'n' I know
'em. Do you think I'm a idgit, Eli?"

"Actin' mighty nateral now." Isom was
raising the pistol again. "Oh, Lawdy!
Don't shoot, boy—don't shoot!"

"Git down on yer knees! Now I want
ye to beg fer mercy thet ye never showed—
thet ye wouldn't 'a' showed Steve. . . .
Purty good," he said, encouragingly.

"Mebbe ye kin pray a leetle, seein' ez
ye air a chu'ch member. Pray fer yer enemies, Eli; Uncl' Gabe says ye must love yer
enemies. I know how ye loves me, 'n' I
want yer to pray fer me. The Lawd mus'

[ 119 ]

sot a powerful store by a good citizen like you. Ax him to fergive me fer killin' ye."

"Have mercy, O Lawd," prayed Crump, to command—and the prayer was subtle— "on the murderer of this thy servant. A life fer a life, thou hev said, O Lawd. Fer killin' me he will foller me, 'n' ef ye hev not mussy he is boun' fer the lowes' pit o' hell, O Lawd——"

It was Isom's time to wince now, and Crump's pious groan was cut short.

"Shet up!" cried the boy, sharply, and he sat a moment silent. "You've been a-spyin' on us sence I was borned, Eli," he said, reflectively. "I believe ye lay-wayed dad. Y'u spied on Rome. Y'u told the soldiers whar he was a-hidin'. Y'u tried to shoot him from the bresh. Y'u found out Steve was goin' to Breathitt on Sunday, 'n' you've jes made a blind to shoot him in

"Pray fer yer enemies, Eli."

the back. I reckon thar's no meanness ye
hain't done. Dad al'ays said ye sot a snare
fer a woman once—a woman! Y'u loaded
a musket with slugs, 'n' tied a string to the
trigger, 'n' stretched hit 'cross the path, 'n'
y'u got up on a cliff 'n' whistled to make
her slow up jes when she struck the string.
I reckon thet's yer wust—but I don't
know."

Several times Crump raised his hands in
protest while his arraignment was going
on; several times he tried to speak, but his
lips refused utterance. The boy's voice
was getting thicker and thicker, and he was
nervously working the cock of the big pistol
up and down.

"Git up," he said; and Crump rose with
a spring. The lad's tone meant release.

"You hain't wuth the risk. I hain't
goin' ter kill ye. I jus' wanted ter banter

ye 'n' make ye beg. You're a good beggar, Eli, 'n' a powerful prayer. You'll be a shinin' light in the chu'ch, ef ye gits a chance ter shine long. Fer lemme tell ye, nobody ever ketched ye afore. But you're ketched now, an' I'm goin' to tell Steve. He'll be a-watchin' fer ye, 'n' so 'll I. I tell ye in time, ef ye ever come over hyeh agin as long as you live, you'll never git back alive. Turn roun'! Hev ye got any balls?" he asked, feeling in Crump's pockets for cartridges. "No; well"—he picked up the Winchester and pumped the magazine empty—"I'll keep these," he said, handing Crump the empty rifle. "Now git away—an' git away quick!"

Crump's slouching footsteps went out of hearing, and Isom sat where he was. His elbows dropped to his knees. His face dropped slowly into his hands, and the nettles of remorse began to sting. He took the back of one tremulous hand presently to wipe the perspiration from his forehead, and he found it burning. A sharp pain shot through his eyes. He knew what that meant, and feeling dizzy, he rose and started a little blindly towards home.

Old Gabe was waiting for him. He did not answer the old man's querulous inquiry, but stumbled towards a bed. An hour later, when the miller was rubbing his forehead, he opened his eyes, shut them, and began to talk.

"I reckon I hain't much better 'n Eli, Uncl' Gabe," he said, plaintively. "I've been abusin' him down thar in the woods. I come might' nigh killin' him onct." The old man stroked on, scarcely heeding the boy's words, so much nonsense would he talk when ill.

[ 123 ]

"I've been lyin' to ye, Uncl' Gabe, 'n'
a-deceivin' of ye right along. Steve's
a-goin' atter ole Brayton—I'm goin' too—
Steve didn't kill Jass—hit wusn't Steve—
hit wusn't Rome—hit was—" The last
word stopped behind his shaking lips; he
rose suddenly in bed, looked wildly into the
miller's startled face, and dropping with a
sob to the bed, went sobbing to sleep.

Old Gabe went back to his pipe, and
while he smoked, his figure shrank slowly in
his chair. He went to bed finally, but sleep
would not come, and he rose again and
built up the fire and sat by it, waiting for
day. His own doctrine, sternly taught for
many a year, had come home to him; and
the miller's face when he opened his door
was gray as the breaking light.

# IV

THERE was little peace for old Gabe that day at the mill. And when he went home at night he found cause for the thousand premonitions that had haunted him. The lad was gone.

A faint light in the east was heralding the moon when Isom reached Steve Marcum's gate. There were several horses hitched to the fence, several dim forms seated in the porch, and the lad hallooed for Steve, whose shadow shot instantly from the door and came towards him.

"Glad ter see ye, Isom," he called, jubilantly. "I was jus' about to sen' fer ye. How'd ye happen to come up?"

Isom answered in a low voice with the

news of Crump's "blind," and Steve laughed and swore in the same breath.

"Come hyeh!" he said, leading the way back; and at the porch he had Isom tell the story again.

"Whut d' I tell ye, boys?" he asked, triumphantly. "Don't believe ye more 'n half believed me."

Three more horsemen rode up to the gate and came into the light. Every man was armed, and at Isom's puzzled look, Steve caught the lad by the arm and led him around the chimney-corner. He was in high spirits.

" 'Pears like ole times, Isom. I'm a-goin' fer thet cussed ole Steve Brayton this very night. He's behind Crump. I s'picioned it afore; now I know it for sartain. He's a-goin' to give Eli a mule 'n' a Winchester fer killin' me. We're goin'

to s'prise him to-night. He won't be look-
in' fer us—I've fixed that. I wus jus'
about to sen' fer ye. I hain't fergot how
ye kin handle a gun." Steve laughed significantly. "Ye're a good frien' o' mine,
'n' I'm goin' to show ye thet I'm a frien'
o' yourn."

Isom's paleness was unnoticed in the
dark. The old throbbing began to beat
again at his temple; the old haze started
from his eyes.

"Hyeh's yer gun, Isom," he heard Steve
saying next. The fire was blazing into his
face. At the chimney-corner was the bent
figure of old Daddy Marcum, and across
his lap shone a Winchester. Steve was
pointing at it, his grim face radiant; the
old man's toothless mouth was grinning,
and his sharp black eyes were snapping up
at him.

"Hit's yourn, I tell ye," said Steve again. "I aimed jes to lend it to ye, but ye've saved me frum gittin' killed, mebbe, 'n' hit's yourn now—yourn, boy, fer keeps."

Steve was holding the gun out to him now. The smooth cold touch of the polished barrel thrilled him. It made everything for an instant clear again, and feeling weak, Isom sat down on the bed, gripping the treasure in both trembling hands. On one side of him some one was repeating Steve's plan of attack. Old Brayton's cabin was nearly opposite, but they would go up the river, cross above the mill, and ride back. The night was cloudy, but they would have the moonlight now and then for the climb up the mountain. They would creep close, and when the moon was hid they would run in and get old Brayton

[ 128 ]

alive, if possible. Then—the rest was with Steve.

Across the room he could hear Steve telling the three new-comers, with an occasional curse, about Crump's blind, and how he knew that old Brayton was hiring Crump.

"Old Steve's meaner 'n Eli," he said to himself, and a flame of the old hate surged up from the fire of temptation in his heart. Steve Marcum was his best friend; Steve had shielded him. The boy had promised to join him against old Brayton, and here was the Winchester, brand-new, to bind his word.

"Git ready, boys; git ready."

It was Steve's voice, and in Isom's ears the preacher's voice rang after it. Again that blinding mist before his eyes, and the boy brushed at it irritably. He could see

[ 129 ]

the men buckling cartridge-belts, but he sat still. Two or three men were going out. Daddy Marcum was leaning on a chair at the door, looking eagerly at each man as he passed.

"Hain't ye goin', Isom?"

Somebody was standing before him twirling a rifle on its butt, a boy near Isom's age. The whirling gun made him dizzy.

"Stop it!" he cried, angrily. Old Daddy Marcum was answering the boy's question from the door.

"Isom goin'?" he piped, proudly. "I reckon he air. Whar's yer belt, boy? Git ready. Git ready."

Isom rose then—he could not answer sitting down—and caught at a bedpost with one hand, while he fumbled at his throat with the other.

"I *hain't* goin'."

Steve heard at the door, and whirled around. Daddy Marcum was tottering across the floor, with one bony hand up-lifted.

"You're a coward!" The name stilled every sound. Isom, with eyes afire, sprang at the old man to strike, but somebody caught his arm and forced him back to the bed.

"Shet up, dad," said Steve, angrily, looking sharply into Isom's face. "Don't ye see the boy's sick? He needn't go ef he don't want to. Time to start, boys."

The tramp of heavy boots started across the puncheon floor and porch again. Isom could hear Steve's orders outside; the laughs and jeers and curses of the men as they mounted their horses; he heard the cavalcade pass through the gate, the old man's cackling good-by; then the horses' hoofs going down the mountain, and Daddy Marcum's hobbling step on the porch again. He was standing in the middle of the floor, full in the firelight, when the old man reached the threshold—standing in a trance, with a cartridge-belt in his hand.

"Good fer you, Isom!"

The cry was apologetic, and stopped short.

"The critter's fersaken," he quavered, and cowed by the boy's strange look, the old man shrank away from him along the wall. But Isom seemed neither to see nor hear. He caught up his rifle, and wavering an instant, tossed it with the belt on the bed and ran out the door. The old man followed, dumb with amazement.

"Isom!" he called, getting his wits and

[ 132 ]

his tongue at last. "Hyeh's yer gun! Come back, I tell ye! You've fergot yer gun! Isom! Isom!"

The voice piped shrilly out into the darkness, and piped back without answer.

A steep path, dangerous even by day, ran snakelike from the cabin down to the water's edge. It was called Isom's path after that tragic night. No mountaineer went down it thereafter without a firm faith that only by the direct help of Heaven could the boy, in his flight down through the dark, have reached the river and the other side alive. The path dropped from ledge to ledge, and ran the brink of precipices and chasms. In a dozen places the boy crashed through the undergrowth from one slippery fold to the next below, catching at roots and stones, slipping past death a score of times, and dropping on till a flood of yellow light lashed the gloom before him. Just there the river was most narrow; the nose of a cliff swerved the current sharply across, and on the other side an eddy ran from it up stream. These earthly helps he had, and he needed them.

There had been a rain-storm, and the waves swept him away like thistle-down, and beat back at him as he fought through them and stood choked and panting on the other shore. He did not dare stop to rest. The Marcums, too, had crossed the river up at the ford by this time, and were galloping towards him; and Isom started on and up. When he reached the first bench of the spur the moon was swinging over Thunderstruck Knob. The clouds broke as he climbed; strips of radiant sky showed between the rolling masses,

[ 134 ]

and the mountain above was light and dark in quick succession. He had no breath when he reached the ledge that ran above old Steve's cabin, and flinging one arm above it, he fell through sheer exhaustion. The cabin was dark as the clump of firs behind it; the inmates were unsuspecting; and Steve Marcum and his men were not far below. A rumbling started under him, while he lay there and grew faint—the rumble of a stone knocked from the path by a horse's hoof. Isom tried to halloo, but his voice stopped in a whisper, and he painfully drew himself upon the rock, upright under the bright moon. A quick oath of warning came then—it was Crump's shrill voice in the Brayton cabin —and Isom stumbled forward with both hands thrown up and a gasping cry at his lips. One flash came through a port-hole

of the cabin. A yell broke on the night—
Crump's cry again—and the boy swayed
across the rock, and falling at the brink,
dropped with a limp struggle out of sight.

## V

THE news of Isom's fate reached the miller by way of Hazlan before the next noon. Several men in the Brayton cabin had recognized the boy in the moonlight. At daybreak they found bloodstains on the ledge and on a narrow shelf a few feet farther down. Isom had slipped from one to the other, they said, and in his last struggle had rolled over into Dead Creek, and had been swept into the Cumberland.

It was Crump who had warned the Braytons. Nobody ever knew how he had learned Steve Marcum's purpose. And old Brayton on his guard and in his own cabin was impregnable. So the Marcums, after a harmless fusillade, had turned back cursing. Mocking shouts followed after them, pistol-shots, even the scraping of a fiddle and shuffling on the ledge. But they kept on, cursing across the river and back to Daddy Marcum, who was standing in the porch, peering for them through the dawn, with a story to tell about Isom.

"The critter was teched in the head," the old man said, and this was what the Braytons too believed. But Steve Marcum, going to search for Isom's body next day, gave old Gabe another theory. He told the miller how Daddy Marcum had called Isom a coward, and Steve said the boy had gone ahead to prove he was no coward.

"He had mighty leetle call to prove it to me. Think o' his takin' ole Brayton all

by hisself!" he said, with a look at the
yellow heaving Cumberland. " 'N', Lord!
think o' his swimmin' that river in the
dark!"

Old Gabe asked a question fiercely then
and demanded the truth, and Steve told
him about the hand-to-hand fight on the
mountain-side, about young Jasper's
treachery, and how the boy, who was
watching the fight, fired just in time to save
Rome. It made all plain at last—Rome's
and Steve's denials, Isom's dinning on that
one theme, and why the boy could not go
to Rome and face Martha, with her own
blood on his hands. Isom's true motive,
too, was plain, and the miller told it
brokenly to Steve, who rode away with a
low whistle to tell it broadcast, and left
the old man rocking his body like a
woman.

An hour later he rode back at a gallop to tell old Gabe to search the river bank below the mill. He did not believe Isom dead. It was just his "feelin'," he said, and one fact, that nobody else thought important—the Brayton canoe was gone.

"Ef he was jus' scamped by a ball," said Steve, "you kin bet he tuk the boat, 'n' he's down thar in the bushes somewhar now waitin' fer dark."

And about dusk, sure enough, old Gabe, wandering hopefully through the thicket below the mill, stumbled over the canoe stranded in the bushes. In the new mud were the tracks of a boy's bare feet leading into the thicket, and the miller made straight for home. When he opened his door he began to shake as if with palsy. A figure was seated on the hearth against the chimney, and the firelight was playing

[ 140 ]

over the face and hair. The lips were
parted, and the head hung limply to the
breast. The clothes were torn to rags,
and one shoulder was bare. Through the
upper flesh of it and close to the neck was
an ugly burrow clotted with blood. The
boy was asleep.

Three nights later, in Hazlan, Sherd
Raines told the people of Isom's flight
down the mountain, across the river, and
up the steep to save his life by losing it.
Before he was done, one gray-headed figure
pressed from the darkness on one side and
stood trembling under the dips. It was
old Steve Brayton, who had fired from
the cabin at Isom, and dropping his Winchester, he stumbled forward with the butt
of his pistol held out to Raines. A Marcum appeared on the other side with the

muzzle of his Winchester down. Raines raised both hands then and imperiously called on every man who had a weapon to come forward and give it up. Like children they came, Marcums and Braytons, piling their arms on the rock before him, shaking hands right and left, and sitting together on the mourner's bench.

Old Brayton was humbled thereafter. He wanted to shake hands with Steve Marcum and make friends. But Steve grinned, and said, "Not yit," and went off into the bushes. A few days later he went to Hazlan of his own accord and gave up his gun to Raines. He wouldn't shake hands with old Brayton, he said, nor with any other man who would hire another man to do his "killin';" but he promised to fight no more, and he kept his word.

A flood followed on New Year's day.
Old Gabe's canoe—his second canoe—was
gone, and a Marcum and a Brayton
worked side by side at the mill hollowing
out another. The miller sat at the door
whittling.

" 'Pears like folks is havin' bad luck
with thar dugouts," said the Brayton.
"Some triflin' cuss took old Steve Brayton's jes to cross the river, without the
grace to tie it to the bank, let 'lone takin'
it back. I've heard ez how Aunt Sally
Day's boy Ben, who was a-fishin' that
evenin', says ez how he seed Isom's harnt
a-floatin' across the river in it, without
techin' a paddle."

The Marcum laughed. "Idgits is thick
over hyeh," he said. "Ben's a-gittin' wuss
sence Isom was killed. Yes, I recollect
Gabe hyeh lost a canoe jus' atter a flood

more'n a year ago, when Rome Stetson 'n' Marthy Lewallen went a-gallivantin' out'n the mountains together. Hyeh's another flood, 'n' old Gabe's dugout gone agin." The miller raised a covert glance of suspicion from under his hat, but the Marcum was laughing. "Ye oughter put a trace-chain on this 'un," he added. "A rope gits rotten in the water, 'n' a tide is mighty apt to break it."

Old Gabe said that "mebbe that wus so," but he had no chain to waste; he reckoned a rope was strong enough, and he started home.

"Old Gabe don't seem to keer much now 'bout Isom," said the Brayton. "Folks say he tuk on so awful at fust that hit looked like he wus goin' crazy. He's gittin' downright peert again. Hello!"

Bud Vickers was carrying a piece of

news down to Hazlan, and he pulled up his horse to deliver it. Aunt Sally Day's dog had been seen playing in the Breathitt road with the frame of a human foot. Some boys had found not far away, behind a withered "blind," a heap of rags and bones. Eli Crump had not been seen in Hazlan since the night of the Brayton raid.

"Well, ef hit was Eli," said the Brayton, waggishly, "we're all goin' to be saved. Eli's case 'll come fust, an' ef thar's only one Jedgment day, the Lord 'll nuver git to us."

The three chuckled, while old Gabe sat dreaming at his gate. The boy had lain quiet during the weeks of his getting well, absorbed in one aim—to keep hidden until he was strong enough to get to Rome. On the last night the miller had raised one of

the old hearth-stones and had given him
the hire of many years. At daybreak the
lad drifted away. Now old Gabe was following him down the river and on to the
dim mountain line, where the boy's figure
was plain for a moment against the sky,
and then was lost.

The clouds in the west had turned gray
and the crescent had broken the gloom of
the woods into shadows when the miller
rose. One star was coming over Black
Mountain from the east. It was the Star
of Bethlehem to old Gabe; and, star-like
on both sides of the Cumberland, answering fires from cabin hearths were giving
back its message at last.

"Thar hain't nothin' to hender Rome
'n' Marthy now. I nuver knowed anybody to stay 'way from these mount'ins ef
he could git back; 'n' Isom said he'd fetch

'em. Thar hain't nothin' to hender—
nothin' now."

On the stoop of the cabin the miller
turned to look again, and then on the last
Stetson the door was closed.

# THE  PARDON  OF  BECKY  DAY

# THE PARDON OF BECKY DAY

THE missionary was young and she was from the North. Her brows were straight, her nose was rather high, and her eyes were clear and gray. The upper lip of her little mouth was so short that the teeth just under it were never quite concealed. It was the mouth of a child and it gave the face, with all its strength and high purpose, a peculiar pathos that no soul in that little mountain town had the power to see or feel. A yellow mule was hitched to the rickety fence in front of her and she stood on the stoop of a little white frame-house with an elm switch between her teeth and gloves on her hands, which were white and looked strong. The mule wore a man's saddle, but no matter— the streets were full of yellow pools, the mud was ankle-deep, and she was on her way to the sick-bed of Becky Day.

There was a flood that morning. All the preceding day the rains had drenched the high slopes unceasingly. That night, the rain-clear forks of the Kentucky got yellow and rose high, and now they crashed together around the town and, after a heaving conflict, started the river on one quivering, majestic sweep to the sea.

Nobody gave heed that the girl rode a mule or that the saddle was not her own, and both facts she herself quickly forgot. This half log, half frame house on a corner had stood a siege once. She could yet see bullet holes about the door. Through

[ 152 ]

this window, a revenue officer from the Blue Grass had got a bullet in the shoulder from a garden in the rear. Standing in the post-office door only just one month before, she herself had seen children scurrying like rabbits through the back-yard fences, men running silently here and there, men dodging into doorways, fire flashing in the street and from every house— and not a sound but the crack of pistol and Winchester; for the mountain men deal death in all the terrible silence of death. And now a preacher with a long scar across his forehead had come to the one little church in the place and the fervor of religion was struggling with feudal hate for possession of the town. To the girl, who saw a symbol in every mood of the earth, the passions of these primitive people were like the treacherous streams of the

[ 153 ]

uplands—now quiet as sunny skies and now clashing together with but little less fury and with much more noise. And the roar of the flood above the wind that late afternoon was the wrath of the Father, that with the peace of the Son so long on earth, such things still could be. Once more trouble was threatening and that day even she knew that trouble might come, but she rode without fear, for she went when and where she pleased as any woman can, throughout the Cumberland, without insult or harm.

At the end of the street were two houses that seemed to front each other with unmistakable enmity. In them were two men who had wounded each other only the day before, and who that day would lead the factions, if the old feud broke loose again. One house was close to the frothing hem

[ 154 ]

of the flood—a log-hut with a shed of rough boards for a kitchen—the home of Becky Day.

The other was across the way and was framed and smartly painted. On the steps sat a woman with her head bare and her hands under her apron—widow of the Marcum whose death from a bullet one month before had broken the long truce of the feud. A groaning curse was growled from the window as the girl drew near, and she knew it came from a wounded Marcum who had lately come back from the West to avenge his brother's death.

"Why don't you go over to see your neighbor?" The girl's clear eyes gave no hint that she knew—as she well did—the trouble between the houses, and the widow stared in sheer amazement, for mountain-

[ 155 ]

eers do not talk with strangers of the quarrels between them.

"I have nothin' to do with such as her," she said, sullenly; "she ain't the kind——"

"Don't!" said the girl, with a flush, "she's dying."

*"Dyin'?"*

"Yes." With the word the girl sprang from the mule and threw the reins over the pale of the fence in front of the log-hut across the way. In the doorway she turned as though she would speak to the woman on the steps again, but a tall man with a black beard appeared in the low door of the kitchen-shed.

"How is your—how is Mrs. Day?"

"Mighty puny this mornin'—Becky is."

The girl slipped into the dark room. On a disordered, pillowless bed lay a white face with eyes closed and mouth slightly

[ 156 ]

open. Near the bed was a low wood fire. On the hearth were several thick cups filled with herbs and heavy fluids and covered with tarpaulin, for Becky's "man" was a teamster. With a few touches of the girl's quick hands, the covers of the bed were smooth, and the woman's eyes rested on the girl's own cloak. With her own handkerchief she brushed the death-damp from the forehead that already seemed growing cold. At her first touch, the woman's eyelids opened and dropped together again. Her lips moved, but no sound came from them.

In a moment the ashes disappeared, the hearth was clean and the fire was blazing. Every time the girl passed the window she saw the widow across the way staring hard at the hut. When she took the ashes into the street, the woman spoke to her.

[ 157 ]

"I can't go to see Becky—she hates me."

"With good reason."

The answer came with a clear sharpness that made the widow start and redden angrily; but the girl walked straight to the gate, her eyes ablaze with all the courage that the mountain woman knew and yet with another courage to which the primitive creature was a stranger — a courage that made the widow lower her own eyes and twist her hands under her apron.

"I want you to come and ask Becky to forgive you."

The woman stared and laughed.

"Forgive me? Becky forgive me? She wouldn't—an' I don't want her—" She could not look up into the girl's eyes; but she pulled a pipe from under the apron,

[ 158 ]

laid it down with a trembling hand and began to rock slightly.

The girl leaned across the gate.

"Look at me!" she said, sharply. The woman raised her eyes, swerved them once, and then in spite of herself, held them steady.

"Listen! Do you want a dying woman's curse?"

It was a straight thrust to the core of a superstitious heart and a spasm of terror crossed the woman's face. She began to wring her hands.

"Come on!" said the girl, sternly, and turned, without looking back, until she reached the door of the hut, where she beckoned and stood waiting, while the woman started slowly and helplessly from the steps, still wringing her hands. Inside, behind her, the wounded Marcum, who

[ 159 ]

had been listening, raised himself on one elbow and looked after her through the window.

"She can't come in—not while I'm in here."

The girl turned quickly. It was Dave Day, the teamster, in the kitchen door, and his face looked blacker than his beard.

"Oh!" she said, simply, as though hurt, and then with a dignity that surprised her, the teamster turned and strode towards the back door.

"But I can git out, I reckon," he said, and he never looked at the widow who had stopped, frightened, at the gate.

"Oh, I can't—I *can't!*" she said, and her voice broke; but the girl gently pushed her to the door, where she stopped again, leaning against the lintel. Across the way, the wounded Marcum, with a scowl of

[ 160 ]

"Listen! Do you want a dying woman's curse?"

wonder, crawled out of his bed and started painfully to the door. The girl saw him and her heart beat fast.

Inside, Becky lay with closed eyes. She stirred uneasily, as though she felt some hated presence, but her eyes stayed fast, for the presence of Death in the room was stronger still.

"Becky!" At the broken cry, Becky's eyes flashed wide and fire broke through the haze that had gathered in them.

"I want ye ter fergive me, Becky."

The eyes burned steadily for a long time. For two days she had not spoken, but her voice came now, as though from the grave.

"You!" she said, and, again, with torturing scorn, "You!" And then she smiled, for she knew why her enemy was there, and her hour of triumph was come.

The girl moved swiftly to the window—
she could see the wounded Marcum slowly
crossing the street, pistol in hand.

"What'd I ever do to you?"

"Nothin', Becky, nothin'."

Becky laughed harshly. "You can tell
the truth—can't ye—to a dyin' woman?"

"Fergive me, Becky!"

A scowling face, tortured with pain, was
thrust into the window.

"Sh-h!" whispered the girl, imperiously,
and the man lifted his heavy eyes, dropped
one elbow on the window-sill and waited.

"You tuk Jim from me!"

The widow covered her face with her
hands, and the Marcum at the window—
brother to Jim, who was dead—lowered
at her, listening keenly.

"An' you got him by lyin' 'bout me.
You tuk him by lyin' 'bout me—didn't

ye? Didn't ye?" she repeated, fiercely, and her voice would have wrung the truth from a stone.

"Yes—Becky—yes!"

"You hear?" cried Becky, turning her eyes to the girl.

"You made him believe an' made ever'body, you could, believe that I was —was *bad*." Her breath got short but the terrible arraignment went on.

"You started this war. My brother wouldn't 'a' shot Jim Marcum if it hadn't been fer you. You killed Jim—your own husband—an' you killed *me*. An' now you want me to fergive you—you!" She raised her right hand as though with it she would hurl the curse behind her lips, and the widow, with a cry, sprang for the bony fingers, catching them in her own hand and falling over on her knees at the bedside.

[ 163 ]

"Don't, Becky, don't—don't—*don't!*"

There was a slight rustle at the back window. At the other, a pistol flashed into sight and dropped again below the sill. Turning, the girl saw Dave's bushy black head—he, too, with one elbow on the sill and the other hand out of sight.

"Shame!" she said, looking from one to the other of the two men, who had learned, at last, the bottom truth of the feud; and then she caught the sick woman's other hand and spoke quickly:

"Hush, Becky," she said; and at the touch of her hand and the sound of her voice, Becky looked confusedly at her and let her upraised hand sink back to the bed. The widow stared swiftly from Jim's brother, at one window, to Dave Day at the other, and hid her face on her arms.

"Remember, Becky—how can you ex-

[ 164 ]

pect forgiveness in another world, unless you forgive in this?"

The woman's brow knitted and she lay quiet. Like the widow who held her hand, the dying woman believed, with never the shadow of a doubt, that somewhere above the stars, a living God reigned in a heaven of never-ending happiness; that somewhere beneath the earth a personal devil gloated over souls in eternal torture; that whether she went above, or below, hung solely on her last hour of contrition; and that in heaven or hell she would know those whom she might meet as surely as she had known them on earth. By and by her face softened and she drew a long breath.

"Jim was a good man," she said. And then after a moment:

"An' I was a good woman"—she turned her eyes towards the girl—"until Jim

married *her*. I didn't keer after that."
Then she got calm, and while she spoke
to the widow, she looked at the girl.

"Will you git up in church an' say before ever'body that you knew I was *good*
when you said I was bad—that you lied
about me?"

"Yes—yes." Still Becky looked at the
girl, who stooped again.

"She will, Becky, I know she will.
Won't you forgive her and leave peace behind you? Dave and Jim's brother are
here—make them shake hands. Won't
you—won't you?" she asked, turning from
one to the other.

Both men were silent.

"Won't you?" she repeated, looking at
Jim's brother.

"I've got nothin' agin Dave. I always
thought that she"—he did not call his

[ 166 ]

brother's wife by name—"caused all this trouble. I've nothin' agin Dave."

The girl turned. "Won't you, Dave?"

"I'm waitin' to hear whut Becky says."

Becky was listening, though her eyes were closed. Her brows knitted painfully. It was a hard compromise that she was asked to make between mortal hate and a love that was more than mortal, but the Plea that has stood between them for nearly twenty centuries prevailed, and the girl knew that the end of the feud was nigh.

Becky nodded.

"Yes, I fergive her, an' I want 'em to shake hands."

But not once did she turn her eyes to the woman whom she forgave, and the hand that the widow held gave back no answering pressure. The faces at the win-

[ 167 ]

dows disappeared, and she motioned for the girl to take her weeping enemy away.

She did not open her eyes when the girl came back, but her lips moved and the girl bent above her.

"I know whar Jim is."

From somewhere outside came Dave's cough, and the dying woman turned her head as though she were reminded of something she had quite forgotten. Then, straightway, she forgot again.

The voice of the flood had deepened. A smile came to Becky's lips—a faint, terrible smile of triumph. The girl bent low and, with a startled face, shrank back.

*"An' I'll—git—thar—first."*

With that whisper went Becky's last breath, but the smile was there, even when her lips were cold.

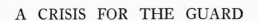

A CRISIS FOR THE GUARD

# A CRISIS FOR THE GUARD

THE tutor was from New England, and he was precisely what passes, with Southerners, as typical. He was thin, he wore spectacles, he talked dreamy abstractions, and he looked clerical. Indeed, his ancestors had been clergymen for generations, and, by nature and principle, he was an apostle of peace and a non-combatant. He had just come to the Gap—a cleft in the Cumberland Mountains—to prepare two young Blue Grass Kentuckians for Harvard. The railroad was still thirty miles away, and he had travelled mule-back through mudholes, on which, as the joke ran, a traveller was supposed to leave his card before he entered and disappeared—that his successor might not unknowingly press him too hard. I do know that, in those mudholes, mules were sometimes drowned. The tutor's gray mule fell over a bank with him, and he would have gone back had he not feared what was behind more than anything that was possible ahead. He was mud-bespattered, sore, tired and dispirited when he reached the Gap, but still plucky and full of business. He wanted to see his pupils at once and arrange his schedule. They came in after supper, and I had to laugh when I saw his mild eyes open. The boys were only fifteen and seventeen, but each had around him a huge revolver and a belt of cartridges, which he unbuckled and laid on the table after shaking hands. The tutor's shining glasses were raised to me for light. I gave it: my brothers had just come in from a little police duty, I explained.

Everybody was a policeman at the Gap, I added; and, naturally, he still looked puzzled; but he began at once to question the boys about their studies, and, in an hour, he had his daily schedule mapped out and submitted to me. I had to cover my mouth with my hand when I came to one item—"Exercise: a walk of half an hour every Wednesday afternoon between five and six"—for the younger, known since at Harvard as the colonel, and known then at the Gap as the Infant of the Guard, winked most irreverently. As he had just come back from a ten-mile chase down the valley on horseback after a bad butcher, and as either was apt to have a like experience any and every day, I was not afraid they would fail to get exercise enough; so I let that item of the tutor pass.

The tutor slept in my room that night,

[ 173 ]

and my four brothers, the eldest of whom was a lieutenant on the police guard, in a room across the hallway. I explained to the tutor that there was much lawlessness in the region; that we "foreigners" were trying to build a town, and that, to ensure law and order, we had all become volunteer policemen. He seemed to think it was most interesting.

About three o'clock in the morning a shrill whistle blew, and, from habit, I sprang out of bed. I had hardly struck the floor when four pairs of heavy boots thundered down the stairs just outside the door, and I heard a gasp from the startled tutor. He was bolt upright in bed, and his face in the moonlight was white with fear.

"Wha—wha—what's that?"

I told him that it was a police whistle and

that the boys were answering it. Everybody jumped when he heard a whistle, I
explained; for nobody in town was permit-
ted to blow one except a policeman. I
guessed there would be enough men answering that whistle without me, however,
and I slipped back into bed.

"Well," he said; and when the boys
lumbered upstairs again and one shouted
through the door, "All right!" the tutor
said again with emphasis: "Well!"

Next day there was to be a political
gathering at the Gap. A Senator was trying to lift himself by his own boot-straps
into the Governor's chair. He was going to
make a speech, there would be a big and
unruly crowd, and it would be a crucial
day for the Guard. So, next morning, I
suggested to the tutor that it would be
unwise for him to begin work with his

pupils that day, for the reason that he was likely to be greatly interrupted and often. He thought, however, he would like to begin. He did begin, and within half an hour Gordon, the town sergeant, thrust his head inside the door and called the colonel by name.

"Come on," he said; "they're going to try that d——n butcher." And seeing from the tutor's face that he had done something dreadful, he slammed the door in apologetic confusion. The tutor was law-abiding, and it was the law that called the colonel, and so the tutor let him go—nay, went with him and heard the case. The butcher had gone off on another man's horse—the man owed him money, he said, and the only way he could get his money was to take the horse as security. But the sergeant did not know this, and he and the

[ 176 ]

colonel rode after him, and the colonel, having the swifter horse, but not having had time to get his own pistol, took the sergeant's and went ahead. He fired quite close to the running butcher twice, and the butcher thought it wise to halt. When he saw the child who had captured him he was speechless, and he got off his horse and cut a big switch to give the colonel a whipping, but the doughty Infant drew down on him again and made him ride, foaming with rage, back to town. The butcher was good-natured at the trial, however, and the tutor heard him say, with a great guffaw:

"An' I *do* believe the d——n little fool would 'a' shot me."

Once more the tutor looked at the pupil whom he was to lead into the classic halls of Harvard, and once more he said:

"Well!"

People were streaming into town now, and I persuaded the tutor that there was no use for him to begin his studies again. He said he would go fishing down the river and take a swim. He would get back in time to hear the speaking in the afternoon. So I got him a horse, and he came out with a long cane fishing-pole and a pair of saddle-bags. I told him that he must watch the old nag or she would run away with him, particularly when he started homeward. The tutor was not much of a centaur. The horse started as he was throwing the wrong leg over his saddle, and the tutor clamped his rod under one arm, clutching for the reins with both hands and kicking for his stirrups with both feet. The tip of the limber pole beat the horse's flank gently as she struck a trot, and smartly as she struck into a lope, and so with arms, feet, saddle-pockets, and fishing-rod flapping towards different points of the compass, the tutor passed out of sight over Poplar Hill on a dead run.

As soon as he could get over a fit of laughter and catch his breath, the colonel asked:

"Do you know what he had in those saddle-pockets?"

"No."

"A bathing suit," he shouted; and he went off again.

Not even in a primeval forest, it seemed, would the modest Puritan bare his body to the mirror of limpid water and the caress of mountain air.

*     *     *     *     *

The trouble had begun early that

[ 179 ]

morning, when Gordon, the town sergeant, stepped from his door and started down the street with no little self-satisfaction. He had been arraying himself for a full hour, and after a tub-bath and a shave he stepped, spic and span, into the street with his head steadily held high, except when he bent it to look at the shine of his boots, which was the work of his own hands, and of which he was proud. As a matter of fact, the sergeant felt that he looked just as he particularly wanted to look on that day—his best. Gordon was a native of Wise, but that day a girl was coming from Lee, and he was ready for her.

Opposite the Intermont, a pistol-shot cracked from Cherokee Avenue, and from habit he started that way. Logan, the captain of the Guard—the leading lawyer in that part of the State—was ahead of him, however, and he called to Gordon to follow. Gordon ran in the grass along the road to keep those boots out of the dust. Somebody had fired off his pistol for fun and was making tracks for the river. As they pushed the miscreant close, he dashed into the river to wade across. It was a very cold morning, and Gordon prayed that the captain was not going to be such a fool as to follow the fellow across the river. He should have known better.

"In with you," said the captain quietly, and the mirror of the shining boots was dimmed, and the icy water chilled the sergeant to the knees and made him so mad that he flashed his pistol and told the runaway to halt, which he did in the middle of the stream. It was Richards, the tough from "the Pocket," and, as he paid his fine promptly, they had to let him go. Gordon went back, put on his everyday clothes and got his billy and his whistle and prepared to see the maid from Lee when his duty should let him. As a matter of fact, he saw her but once, and then he was not made happy.

The people had come in rapidly—giants from the Crab Orchard, mountaineers from through the Gap, and from Cracker's Neck and Thunderstruck Knob; Valley people from Little Stone Gap, from the furnace site and Bum Hollow and Wildcat, and people from Lee, from Turkey Cove, and from the Pocket—the much-dreaded Pocket—far down in the river hills.

They came on foot and on horseback, and left their horses in the bushes and crowded the streets and filled the saloon

[ 182 ]

of one Jack Woods—who had the cackling laugh of Satan and did not like the Guard, for good reasons, and whose particular pleasure was to persuade some customer to stir up a hornet's nest of trouble. From the saloon the crowd moved up towards the big spring at the foot of Imboden Hill, where, under beautiful trunk-mottled beeches, was built the speakers' platform.

Precisely at three o'clock the local orator, much flurried, rose, ran his hand through his long hair and looked in silence over the crowd.

"Fellow citizens! There's beauty in the stars of night and in the glowin' orb of day. There's beauty in the rollin' meadow and in the quiet stream. There's beauty in the smilin' valley and in the everlastin' hills. Therefore, fellow citizens—THERE-FORE, fellow citizens, allow me to intro-

[ 183 ]

duce to you the future Governor of these United States—Senator William Bayhone." And he sat down with such a beatific smile of self-satisfaction that a fiend would not have had the heart to say he had not won.

Now, there are wandering minstrels yet in the Cumberland Hills. They play fiddles and go about making up "ballets" that involve local history. Sometimes they make a pretty good verse—this, for instance, about a feud:

> The death of these two men
>> Caused great trouble in our land.
> Caused men to leave their families
>> And take the parting hand.
> Retaliation, still at war,
>> May never, never cease.
> I would that I could only see
>> Our land once more at peace.

There was a minstrel out in the crowd, and pretty soon he struck up his fiddle and his lay, and he did not exactly sing the virtues of Billy Bayhone. Evidently some partisan thought he ought, for he smote him on the thigh with the toe of his boot and raised such a stir as a rude stranger might had he smitten a troubadour in Arthur's Court. The crowd thickened and surged, and four of the Guard emerged with the fiddler and his assailant under arrest. It was as though the Valley were a sheet of water straightway and the fiddler the dropping of a stone, for the ripple of mischief started in every direction. It caught two mountaineers on the edge of the crowd, who for no particular reason thumped each other with their huge fists, and were swiftly led away by that silent Guard. The operation of a mysterious

[ 185 ]

force was in the air and it puzzled the crowd. Somewhere a whistle would blow, and, from this point and that, a quiet, well-dressed young man would start swiftly toward it. The crowd got restless and uneasy, and, by and by, experimental and defiant. For in that crowd was the spirit of Bunker Hill and King's Mountain. It couldn't fiddle and sing; it couldn't settle its little troubles after the good old fashion of fist and skull; it couldn't charge up and down the streets on horseback if it pleased; it couldn't ride over those puncheon sidewalks; it could't drink openly and without shame; and, Shades of the American Eagle and the Stars and Stripes, it couldn't even yell! No wonder, like the heathen, it raged. What did these blanked "furriners" have against them anyhow? They couldn't run *their* country—not much.

[ 186 ]

Pretty soon there came a shrill whistle
far down-town—then another and another.
It sounded ominous, indeed, and it was,
being a signal of distress from the Infant
of the Guard, who stood before the door
of Jack Woods's saloon with his pistol
levelled on Richards, the tough from the
Pocket—the Infant, standing there with
blazing eyes, alone and in the heart of a
gathering storm.

Now the chain of lawlessness that had
tightened was curious and significant.
There was the tough and his kind—law-
less, irresponsible and possible in any com-
munity. There was the farm-hand who
had come to town with the wild son of his
employer—an honest, law-abiding farmer.
Came, too, a friend of the farmer who
had not yet reaped the crop of wild oats
sown in his youth. Whiskey ran all into

[ 187 ]

one mould. The farm-hand drank with
the tough, the wild son with the farm-
hand, and the three drank together, and
got the farmer's unregenerate friend to
drink with them; and he and the law-abiding farmer himself, by and by, took a drink
for old time's sake. Now the cardinal
command of rural and municipal districts
all through the South is, "Forsake not your
friend": and it does not take whiskey long
to make friends. Jack Woods had given
the tough from the Pocket a whistle.

"You dassen't blow it," said he.

Richards asked why, and Jack told him.
Straightway the tough blew the whistle,
and when the little colonel ran down to arrest him he laughed and resisted, and the
wild son and the farm-hand and Jack
Woods showed an inclination to take his
part. So, holding his "drop" on the

tough with one hand, the Infant blew vigorously for help with the other.

Logan, the captain, arrived first—he usually arrived first—and Gordon, the sergeant, was by his side—Gordon was always by his side. He would have stormed a battery if the captain had led him, and the captain would have led him—alone— if he thought it was his duty. Logan was as calm as a stage hero at the crisis of a play. The crowd had pressed close.

"Take that man," he said sharply, pointing to the tough whom the colonel held covered, and two men seized him from behind.

The farm-hand drew his gun.

"No, you don't!" he shouted.

"Take *him*," said the captain quietly; and he was seized by two more and disarmed.

[ 189 ]

It was then that Sturgeon, the wild son, ran up.

"You can't take that man to jail," he shouted with an oath, pointing at the farm-hand.

The captain waved his hand. "And *him!*"

As two of the Guard approached, Sturgeon started for his gun. Now, Sturgeon was Gordon's blood cousin, but Gordon levelled his own pistol. Sturgeon's weapon caught in his pocket, and he tried to pull it loose. The moment he succeeded Gordon stood ready to fire. Twice the hammer of the sergeant's pistol went back almost to the turning-point, and then, as he pulled the trigger again, Macfarlan, first lieutenant, who once played lacrosse at Yale, rushed, parting the crowd right and left, and dropped his billy lightly three times—right, left and right—on Sturgeon's head. The blood spurted, the head fell back between the bully's shoulders, his grasp on his pistol loosened, and he sank to his knees. For a moment the crowd was stunned by the lightning quickness of it all. It was the first blow ever struck in that country with a piece of wood in the name of the law.

"Take 'em on, boys," called the captain, whose face had paled a little, though he seemed as cool as ever.

And the boys started, dragging the three struggling prisoners, and the crowd, growing angrier and angrier, pressed close behind, a hundred of them, led by the farmer himself, a giant in size, and beside himself with rage and humiliation. Once he broke through the guard line and was pushed back. Knives and pistols began to

[ 191 ]

flash now everywhere, and loud threats and curses rose on all sides—the men should not be taken to jail. The sergeant, dragging Sturgeon, looked up into the blazing eyes of a girl on the sidewalk, Sturgeon's sister—the maid from Lee. The sergeant groaned. Logan gave some order just then to the Infant, who ran ahead, and by the time the Guard with the prisoners had backed to a corner there were two lines of Guards drawn across the street. The first line let the prisoners and their captors through, closed up behind, and backed slowly towards the corner, where it meant to stand.

It was very exciting there. Winchesters and shotguns protruded from the line threateningly, but the mob came on as though it were going to press through, and determined faces blenched with ex-

[ 192 ]

The sergeant, dragging Sturgeon, looked up into the blazing eyes of a girl on the sidewalk.

citement, but not with fear. A moment later, the little colonel and the Guards on either side of him were jabbing at men with cocked Winchesters. At that moment it would have needed but one shot to ring out to have started an awful carnage; but not yet was there a man in the mob—and that is the trouble with mobs—who seemed willing to make a sacrifice of himself that the others might gain their end. For one moment they halted, cursing and waving their pistols, preparing for a charge; and in that crucial moment the tutor from New England came like a thunderbolt to the rescue. Shrieks of terror from children, shrieks of outraged modesty from women, rent the air down the street where the huddled crowd was rushing right and left in wild confusion, and, through the parting crowd, the tutor flew

[ 193 ]

into sight on horseback, bareheaded, barefooted, clad in a gaudily striped bathing
suit, with his saddle-pockets flapping behind him like wings. Some mischievous
mountaineers, seeing him in his bathing
suit on the point of a rock up the river,
had joyously taken a pot-shot or two at
him, and the tutor had mounted his horse
and fled. But he came as welcome and as
effective as an emissary straight from the
God of Battles, though he came against his
will, for his old nag was frantic and was
running away. Men, women and children
parted before him, and gaping mouths
widened as he passed. The impulse of the
crowd ran faster than his horse, and even
the enraged mountaineers in amazed wonder sprang out of his way, and, far in the
rear, a few privileged ones saw the frantic
horse plunge towards his stable, stop sud-

[ 194 ]

denly, and pitch his mottled rider through the door and mercifully out of sight. Human purpose must give way when a pure miracle comes to earth to baffle it. It gave way now long enough to let the oaken doors of the calaboose close behind tough, farm-hand, and the farmer's wild son. The line of Winchesters at the corner quietly gave way. The power of the Guard was established, the backbone of the opposition broken; henceforth, the work for law and order was to be easy compared with what it had been. Up at the big spring under the beeches sat the disgusted orator of the day and the disgusted Senator, who, seriously, was quite sure that the Guard, being composed of Democrats, had taken this way to shatter his campaign.

\*        \*        \*        \*        \*

Next morning, in court, the members of the Guard acted as witnesses against the culprits. Macfarlan stated that he had struck Sturgeon over the head to save his life, and Sturgeon, after he had paid his fine, said he would prefer being shot to being clubbed to death, and he bore dangerous malice for a long time, until he learned what everybody else knew, that Macfarlan always did what he thought he ought, and never spoke anything but the literal truth, whether it hurt friend, foe or himself.

After court, Richards, the tough, met Gordon, the sergeant, in the road. "Gordon," he said, "you swore to a —— lie about me a while ago."

"How do you want to fight?" asked Gordon.

"Fair!"

"Come on;" and Gordon started for the town limits across the river, Richards following on horseback. At a store, Gordon unbuckled his belt and tossed his pistol and his police badge inside. Jack Woods, seeing this, followed, and the Infant, seeing Woods, followed too. The law was law, but this affair was personal, and would be settled without the limits of law and local obligation. Richards tried to talk to Gordon, but the sergeant walked with his head down, as though he could not hear—he was too enraged to talk.

While Richards was hitching his horse in the bushes the sergeant stood on the bank of the river with his arms folded and his chin swinging from side to side. When he saw Richards in the open he rushed for him like a young bull that feels the first swelling of his horns. It was not a fair,

[ 197 ]

stand-up, knock-down English fight, but a Scotch tussle, in which either could strike, kick, bite or gouge. After a few blows they clinched and whirled and fell, Gordon on top—with which advantage he began to pound the tough from the Pocket savagely. Woods made as if to pull him off, but the Infant drew his pistol. "Keep off!"

"He's killing him!" shouted Woods, halting.

"Let him holler 'Enough,' then," said the Infant.

"He's killing him!" shouted Woods.

"Let Gordon's friends take him off, then," said the Infant. "Don't *you* touch him."

And it was done. Richards was senseless and speechless—he really couldn't shout "Enough." But he was content, and the day left a very satisfactory impression

on him and on his friends. If they mis-
behaved in town they would be arrested:
that was plain. But it was also plain that
if anybody had a personal grievance
against one of the Guard he could call him
out of the town limits and get satisfaction,
after the way of his fathers. There was
nothing personal at all in the attitude of
the Guard towards the outsiders; which
recognition was a great stride toward
mutual understanding and final high re-
gard.

All that day I saw that something was
troubling the tutor from New England.
It was the Moral Sense of the Puritan at
work, I supposed, and, that night, when
I came in with a new supply of "billies"
and gave one to each of my brothers, the
tutor looked up over his glasses and
cleared his throat.

"Now," said I to myself, "we shall

catch it hot on the savagery of the South and the barbarous Method of keeping it down;" but before he had said three words the colonel looked as though he were going to get up and slap the little dignitary on the back—which would have created a sensation indeed.

"Have you an extra one of those— those——"

"Billies?" I said, wonderingly.

"Yes. I—I believe I shall join the Guard myself," said the tutor from New England.

# CHRISTMAS NIGHT WITH SATAN

# CHRISTMAS NIGHT WITH
# SATAN

NO night was this in Hades with solemn-eyed Dante, for Satan was only a woolly little black dog, and surely no dog was ever more absurdly misnamed. When Uncle Carey first heard that name, he asked gravely:

"Why, Dinnie, where in h——," Uncle Carey gulped slightly, "did you get him?" And Dinnie laughed merrily, for she saw the fun of the question, and shook her black curls.

"He didn't come f'um *that place*."

Distinctly Satan had not come from that place. On the contrary, he might by

a miracle have dropped straight from
some Happy Hunting-Ground, for all the
signs he gave of having touched pitch in
this or another sphere.  Nothing human
was ever born that was gentler, merrier,
more trusting or more lovable than Satan.
That was why Uncle Carey said again
gravely that he could hardly tell Satan
and his little mistress apart.  He rarely
saw them apart, and as both had black
tangled hair and bright black eyes; as one
awoke every morning with a happy smile
and the other with a jolly bark; as they
played all day like wind-shaken shadows
and each won every heart at first sight—
the likeness was really rather curious.  I
have always believed that Satan made the
spirit of Dinnie's house, orthodox and
severe though it was, almost kindly toward
his great namesake.  I know I have never

[ 204 ]

been able, since I knew little Satan, to think old Satan as bad as I once painted him, though I am sure the little dog had many pretty tricks that the "old boy" doubtless has never used in order to amuse his friends.

"Shut the door, Saty, please," Dinnie would say, precisely as she would say it to Uncle Billy, the butler, and straight-way Satan would launch himself at it— bang! He never would learn to close it softly, for Satan liked that—bang!

If you kept tossing a coin or marble in the air, Satan would keep catching it and putting it back in your hand for another throw, till you got tired. Then he would drop it on a piece of rag carpet, snatch the carpet with his teeth, throw the coin across the room and rush for it like mad, until he got tired. If you put a penny on his nose, he would wait until you counted, one—two—*three!* Then he would toss it up himself and catch it. Thus, perhaps, Satan grew to love Mammon right well, but for another and better reason than that he liked simply to throw it around— as shall now be made plain.

A rubber ball with a hole in it was his favorite plaything, and he would take it in his mouth and rush around the house like a child, squeezing it to make it whistle. When he got a new ball, he would hide his old one away until the new one was the worse worn of the two, and then he would bring out the old one again. If Dinnie gave him a nickel or a dime, when they went down-town, Satan would rush into a store, rear up on the counter where the rubber balls were kept, drop the coin, and get a ball for himself. Thus, Satan learned

Satan would drop the coin and get a ball for himself.

finance. He began to hoard his pennies, and one day Uncle Carey found a pile of seventeen under a corner of the carpet. Usually he carried to Dinnie all coins that he found in the street, but he showed one day that he was going into the ball-business for himself. Uncle Carey had given Dinnie a nickel for some candy, and, as usual, Satan trotted down the street behind her. As usual, Satan stopped before the knick-knack shop.

"Tum on, Saty," said Dinnie. Satan reared against the door as he always did, and Dinnie said again:

"Tum on, Saty." As usual, Satan dropped to his haunches, but what was unusual, he failed to bark. Now Dinnie had got a new ball for Satan only that morning, so Dinnie stamped her foot.

"I tell you to tum on, Saty." Satan

[ 207 ]

never moved. He looked at Dinnie as much as to say:

"I have never disobeyed you before, little mistress, but this time I have an excellent reason for what must seem to you very bad manners—" and being a gentleman withal, Satan rose on his haunches and begged.

"You're des a pig, Saty," said Dinnie, but with a sigh for the candy that was not to be, Dinnie opened the door, and Satan, to her wonder, rushed to the counter, put his forepaws on it, and dropped from his mouth a dime. Satan had found that coin on the street. He didn't bark for change, nor beg for two balls, but he had got it in his woolly little head, somehow, that in that store a coin meant a ball, though never before nor afterward did he try to get a ball for a penny.

[ 208 ]

Satan slept in Uncle Carey's room, for of all people, after Dinnie, Satan loved Uncle Carey best. Every day at noon he would go to an upstairs window and watch the cars come around the corner, until a very tall, square-shouldered young man swung to the ground, and down Satan would scamper—yelping—to meet him at the gate. If Uncle Carey, after supper and when Dinnie was in bed, started out of the house, still in his business clothes, Satan would leap out before him, knowing that he too might be allowed to go; but if Uncle Carey had put on black clothes that showed a big, dazzling shirt-front, and picked up his high hat, Satan would sit perfectly still and look disconsolate; for as there were no parties or theatres for Dinnie, so there were none for him. But no matter how late it was when Uncle

[ 209 ]

Carey came home, he always saw Satan's little black nose against the window-pane and heard his bark of welcome.

After intelligence, Satan's chief trait was lovableness—nobody ever knew him to fight, to snap at anything, or to get angry; after lovableness, it was politeness. If he wanted something to eat, if he wanted Dinnie to go to bed, if he wanted to get out of the door, he would beg— beg prettily on his haunches, his little red tongue out and his funny little paws hanging loosely. Indeed, it was just because Satan was so little less than human, I suppose, that old Satan began to be afraid he might have a soul. So the wicked old namesake with the Hoofs and Horns laid a trap for little Satan, and, as he is apt to do, he began laying it early—long, indeed, before Christmas.

When Dinnie started to kindergarten that autumn, Satan found that there was one place where he could never go. Like the lamb, he could not go to school; so while Dinnie was away, Satan began to make friends. He would bark, "Howdy-do?" to every dog that passed his gate. Many stopped to rub noses with him through the fence—even Hugo the mastiff, and nearly all, indeed, except one strange-looking dog that appeared every morning at precisely nine o'clock and took his stand on the corner. There he would lie patiently until a funeral came along, and then Satan would see him take his place at the head of the procession; and thus he would march out to the cemetery and back again. Nobody knew where he came from nor where he went, and Uncle Carey called him the "funeral dog" and

[ 211 ]

said he was doubtless looking for his dead master. Satan even made friends with a scrawny little yellow dog that followed an old drunkard around—a dog that, when his master fell in the gutter, would go and catch a policeman by the coat-tail, lead the officer to his helpless master, and spend the night with him in jail.

By and by Satan began to slip out of the house at night, and Uncle Billy said he reckoned Satan had "jined de club"; and late one night, when he had not come in, Uncle Billy told Uncle Carey that it was "powerful slippery and he reckoned they'd better send de kerridge after him" —an innocent remark that made Uncle Carey send a boot after the old butler, who fled chuckling down the stairs, and left Uncle Carey chuckling in his room.

Satan had "jined de club"—the big club

—and no dog was too lowly in Satan's eyes for admission; for no priest ever preached the brotherhood of man better than Satan lived it—both with man and dog. And thus he lived it that Christmas night—to his sorrow.

Christmas Eve had been gloomy—the gloomiest of Satan's life. Uncle Carey had gone to a neighboring town at noon. Satan had followed him down to the station, and when the train started, Uncle Carey had ordered him to go home. Satan took his time about going home, not knowing it was Christmas Eve. He found strange things happening to dogs that day. The truth was, that policemen were shooting all dogs found that were without a collar and a license, and every now and then a bang and a howl somewhere would stop Satan in his tracks. At a little yellow house

[ 213 ]

on the edge of town he saw half a dozen strange dogs in a kennel, and every now and then a negro would lead a new one up to the house and deliver him to a big man at the door, who, in return, would drop something into the negro's hand. While Satan waited, the old drunkard came along with his little dog at his heels, paused before the door, looked a moment at his faithful follower, and went slowly on. Satan little knew the old drunkard's temptation, for in that yellow house kind-hearted people had offered fifteen cents for each dog brought to them, without a license, that they might mercifully put it to death, and fifteen cents was the precise price for a drink of good whiskey. Just then there was another bang and another howl somewhere, and Satan trotted home to meet a calamity. Dinnie was gone. Her mother

[ 214 ]

had taken her out in the country to Grandmother Dean's to spend Christmas, as was
the family custom, and Mrs. Dean would
not wait any longer for Satan; so she
told Uncle Billy to bring him out after
supper.

"Ain't you 'shamed o' yo'self—suh—?"
said the old butler, "keepin' me from
ketchin' Christmas gifts dis day?"

Uncle Billy was indignant, for the ne-
groes begin at four o'clock in the afternoon
of Christmas Eve to slip around corners
and jump from hiding places to shout
"Christmas Gif'—Christmas Gif' "; and
the one who shouts first gets a gift. No
wonder it was gloomy for Satan—Uncle
Carey, Dinnie, and all gone, and not a
soul but Uncle Billy in the big house.
Every few minutes he would trot on his
little black legs upstairs and downstairs,

[ 215 ]

looking for his mistress. As dusk came on, he would every now and then howl plaintively. After begging his supper, and while Uncle Billy was hitching up a horse in the stable, Satan went out in the yard and lay with his nose between the close panels of the fence—quite heart-broken. When he saw his old friend, Hugo the mastiff, trotting into the gaslight, he began to bark his delight frantically. The big mastiff stopped and nosed his sympathy through the fence for a moment and walked slowly on, Satan frisking and barking along inside. At the gate Hugo stopped, and raising one huge paw, playfully struck it. The gate flew open, and with a happy yelp Satan leaped into the street. The noble mastiff hesitated as though this were not quite regular. He did not belong to the club, and he didn't know that Satan had

[ 216 ]

ever been away from home after dark
in his life. For a moment he seemed to
wait for Dinnie to call him back as she
always did, but this time there was no
sound, and Hugo walked majestically on,
with absurd little Satan running in a circle
about him. On the way they met the
"funeral dog," who glanced inquiringly
at Satan, shied from the mastiff, and trotted on. On the next block the old drunkard's yellow cur ran across the street, and
after interchanging the compliments of
the season, ran back after his staggering
master. As they approached the railroad
track a strange dog joined them, to whom
Hugo paid no attention. At the crossing
another new acquaintance bounded toward
them. This one—a half-breed shepherd
—was quite friendly, and he received Satan's advances with affable condescension.

[ 217 ]

Then another came and another, and little Satan's head got quite confused. They were a queer-looking lot of curs and half-breeds from the negro settlement at the edge of the woods, and though Satan had little experience, his instincts told him that all was not as it should be, and had he been human he would have wondered very much how they had escaped the carnage that day. Uneasy, he looked around for Hugo; but Hugo had disappeared. Once or twice Hugo had looked around for Satan, and Satan paying no attention, the mastiff trotted on home in disgust. Just then a powerful yellow cur sprang out of the darkness over the railroad track, and Satan sprang to meet him, and so nearly had the life scared out of him by the snarl and flashing fangs of the new-comer that he hardly had the strength to shrink back

[ 218 ]

behind his new friend, the half-breed shepherd.

A strange thing then happened. The
other dogs became suddenly quiet, and
every eye was on the yellow cur. He
sniffed the air once or twice, gave two or
three peculiar low growls, and all those
dogs except Satan lost the civilization of
centuries and went back suddenly to the
time when they were wolves and were looking for a leader. The cur was Lobo for
that little pack, and after a short parley,
he lifted his nose high and started away
without looking back, while the other dogs
silently trotted after him. With a mystified yelp, Satan ran after them. The cur
did not take the turnpike, but jumped the
fence into a field, making his way by the
rear of houses, from which now and then
another dog would slink out and silently

[ 219 ]

join the band. Every one of them Satan nosed most friendlily, and to his great joy the funeral dog, on the edge of town, leaped into their midst. Ten minutes later the cur stopped in the midst of some woods, as though he would inspect his followers. Plainly, he disapproved of Satan, and Satan kept out of his way. Then he sprang into the turnpike and the band trotted down it, under flying black clouds and shifting bands of brilliant moonlight. Once, a buggy swept past them. A familiar odor struck Satan's nose, and he stopped for a moment to smell the horse's tracks; and right he was, too, for out at her grandmother's Dinnie refused to be comforted, and in that buggy was Uncle Billy going back to town after him.

Snow was falling. It was a great lark for Satan. Once or twice, as he trotted along, he had to bark his joy aloud, and each time the big cur gave him such a fierce growl that he feared thereafter to open his jaws. But he was happy for all that, to be running out into the night with such a lot of funny friends and not to know or care where he was going. He got pretty tired presently, for over hill and down hill they went, at that unceasing trot, trot, trot! Satan's tongue began to hang out. Once he stopped to rest, but the loneliness frightened him and he ran on after them with his heart almost bursting. He was about to lie right down and die, when the cur stopped, sniffed the air once or twice, and with those same low growls, led the marauders through a rail fence into the woods, and lay quietly down. How Satan loved that soft, thick grass, all snowy that it was! It was almost as good

[ 221 ]

as his own bed at home. And there they lay—how long, Satan never knew, for he went to sleep and dreamed that he was after a rat in the barn at home; and he yelped in his sleep, which made the cur lift his big yellow head and show his fangs. The moving of the half-breed shepherd and the funeral dog waked him at last, and Satan got up. Half crouching, the cur was leading the way toward the dark, still woods on top of the hill, over which the Star of Bethlehem was lowly sinking, and under which lay a flock of the gentle creatures that seemed to have been almost sacred to the Lord of that Star. They were in sore need of a watchful shepherd now. Satan was stiff and chilled, but he was rested and had had his sleep, and he was just as ready for fun as he always was. He didn't understand that sneaking. Why

[ 222 ]

they didn't all jump and race and bark as
he wanted to, he couldn't see; but he was
too polite to do otherwise than as they
did, and so he sneaked after them; and
one would have thought he knew, as well
as the rest, the hellish mission on which
they were bent.

Out of the woods they went, across a
little branch, and there the big cur lay flat
again in the grass. A faint bleat came
from the hill-side beyond, where Satan
could see another woods—and then another bleat, and another. And the cur began to creep again, like a snake in the
grass; and the others crept too, and little
Satan crept, though it was all a sad mys-
tery to him. Again the cur lay still, but
only long enough for Satan to see curious,
fat, white shapes above him—and then,
with a blood-curdling growl, the big brute

[ 223 ]

dashed forward. Oh, there was fun in them after all! Satan barked joyfully. Those were some new playmates—those fat, white, hairy things up there; and Satan was amazed when, with frightened snorts, they fled in every direction. But this was a new game, perhaps, of which he knew nothing, and as did the rest, so did Satan. He picked out one of the white things and fled barking after it. It was a little fellow that he was after, but little as he was, Satan might never have caught up, had not the sheep got tangled in some brush. Satan danced about him in mad glee, giving him a playful nip at his wool and springing back to give him another nip, and then away again. Plainly, he was not going to bite back, and when the sheep struggled itself tired and sank down in a heap, Satan came close and licked him, and as he was

[ 224 ]

very warm and woolly, he lay down and snuggled up against him for awhile, listening to the turmoil that was going on around him. And as he listened, he got frightened.

If this was a new game it was certainly a very peculiar one—the wild rush, the bleats of terror, gasps of agony, and the fiendish growls of attack and the sounds of ravenous gluttony. With every hair bristling, Satan rose and sprang from the woods—and stopped with a fierce tingling of the nerves that brought him horror and fascination. One of the white shapes lay still before him. There was a great steaming red splotch on the snow, and a strange odor in the air that made him dizzy; but only for a moment. Another white shape rushed by. A tawny streak followed, and then, in a patch of moonlight, Satan saw

[ 225 ]

the yellow cur with his teeth fastened in the throat of his moaning playmate. Like lightning Satan sprang at the cur, who tossed him ten feet away and went·back to his awful work. Again Satan leaped, but just then a shout rose behind him, and the cur leaped too as though a bolt of lightning had crashed over him, and, no longer noticing Satan or sheep, began to quiver with fright and slink away. Another shout rose from another direction—another from another.

"Drive 'em into the barn-yard!" was the cry.

Now and then there was a fearful bang and a howl of death-agony, as some dog tried to break through the encircling men, who yelled and cursed as they closed in on the trembling brutes that slunk together and crept on; for it is said, every sheep-killing dog knows his fate if caught, and will make little effort to escape. With them went Satan, through the barn-yard gate, where they huddled in a corner—a shamed and terrified group. A tall overseer stood at the gate.

"Ten of 'em!" he said grimly.

He had been on the lookout for just such a tragedy, for there had recently been a sheep-killing raid on several farms in that neighborhood, and for several nights he had had a lantern hung out on the edge of the woods to scare the dogs away; but a drunken farm-hand had neglected his duty that Christmas Eve.

"Yassuh, an' dey's jus' sebenteen dead sheep out dar," said a negro.

"Look at the little one," said a tall boy who looked like the overseer; and Satan knew that he spoke of him.

[ 227 ]

"Go back to the house, son," said the overseer, "and tell your mother to give you a Christmas present I got for you yesterday." With a glad whoop the boy dashed away, and in a moment dashed back with a brand-new .32 Winchester in his hand.

The dark hour before dawn was just breaking on Christmas Day. It was the hour when Satan usually rushed upstairs to see if his little mistress was asleep. If he were only at home now, and if he only had known how his little mistress was weeping for him amid her playthings and his—two new balls and a brass-studded collar with a silver plate on which was his name, Satan Dean; and if Dinnie could have seen him now, her heart would have broken; for the tall boy raised his gun. There was a jet of smoke, a sharp, clean crack, and the funeral dog started on the right way at last toward his dead master. Another crack, and the yellow cur leaped from the ground and fell kicking. Another crack and another, and with each crack a dog tumbled, until little Satan sat on his haunches amid the writhing pack, alone. His time was now come. As the rifle was raised, he heard up at the big house the cries of children; the popping of fire-crackers; tooting of horns and whistles and loud shouts of "Christmas Gif', Christmas Gif'!" His little heart beat furiously. Perhaps he knew just what he was doing; perhaps it was the accident of habit; most likely Satan simply wanted to go home—but when that gun rose, Satan rose too, on his haunches, his tongue out, his black eyes steady and his funny little paws hanging loosely—and begged! The boy lowered the gun.

"Down, sir!" Satan dropped obediently, but when the gun was lifted again, Satan rose again, and again he begged.

"Down, I tell you!" This time Satan would not down, but sat begging for his life. The boy turned.

"Papa, I can't shoot that dog." Perhaps Satan had reached the stern old overseer's heart. Perhaps he remembered suddenly that it was Christmas. At any rate, he said gruffly:

"Well, let him go."

"Come here, sir!" Satan bounded toward the tall boy, frisking and trustful and begged again.

"Go home, sir!"

Satan needed no second command. Without a sound he fled out the barn-yard, and, as he swept under the front gate, a little girl ran out of the front door of the

[ 230 ]

"Papa, I can't shoot that dog."

big house and dashed down the steps, shrieking:

"Saty! Saty! Oh, Saty!" But Satan never heard. On he fled, across the crisp fields, leaped the fence and struck the road, lickety-split! for home, while Dinnie dropped sobbing in the snow.

"Hitch up a horse, quick," said Uncle Carey, rushing after Dinnie and taking her up in his arms. Ten minutes later, Uncle Carey and Dinnie, both warmly bundled up, were after flying Satan. They never caught him until they reached the hill on the outskirts of town, where was the kennel of the kind-hearted people who were giving painless death to Satan's four-footed kind, and where they saw him stop and turn from the road. There was divine providence in Satan's flight for one little dog that Christmas morning; for

[ 231 ]

Uncle Carey saw the old drunkard staggering down the road without his little
companion, and a moment later, both he
and Dinnie saw Satan nosing a little yellow cur between the palings. Uncle Carey
knew the little cur, and while Dinnie was
shrieking for Satan, he was saying under
his breath:

"Well, I swear!—I swear!—I swear!"
And while the big man who came to the
door was putting Satan into Dinnie's arms,
he said sharply:

"Who brought that yellow dog here?"
The man pointed to the old drunkard's
figure turning a corner at the foot of the
hill.

"I thought so; I thought so. He sold
him to you for—for a drink of whiskey."

The man whistled.

"Bring him out. I'll pay his license."

[ 232 ]

So back went Satan and the little cur to Grandmother Dean's—and Dinnie cried when Uncle Carey told her why he was taking the little cur along. With her own hands she put Satan's old collar on the little brute, took him to the kitchen, and fed him first of all. Then she went into the breakfast-room.

"Uncle Billy," she said severely, "didn't I tell you not to let Saty out?"

"Yes, Miss Dinnie," said the old butler.

"Didn't I tell you I was goin' to whoop you if you let Saty out?"

"Yes, Miss Dinnie."

Miss Dinnie pulled forth from her Christmas treasures a toy riding-whip and the old darky's eyes began to roll in mock terror.

"I'm sorry, Uncle Billy, but I des got to whoop you a little."

[ 233 ]

"Let Uncle Billy off, Dinnie," said Uncle Carey, "this is Christmas."

"All wite," said Dinnie, and she turned to Satan.

In his shining new collar and innocent as a cherub, Satan sat on the hearth begging for his breakfast.